I0761945

SLICK FILTH.

A STORY OF
Robert Walpole
and Henry Giffard

*
* *

to which is appended
THE FARCE OF
The Golden Rump

by
erAto

Printed for Alumbra Publishing.

MMXX

SLICK FILTH.

ll which I tell took place in the Year of our Lord *MDCCXXXVII*.

It is known that, then as much as now, Sir *Robert Walpole* was the King's favourite Minifter — nicknamed the *Prime Minifter* by his Enemies, due to his Excefs of Influence. Yet that Influence was a Neceffity: for the *German*-born King, *George I*, did not know enough of *Englifh* Politicks, to be able to govern the Country without Affiftance. It had been neceffary that fome one ftep in to ferve the Needs of his Majefty. That Man who was able to beft ferve, happened to be a Man of no Rank, and who had formerly been imprifon'd in the *Tower*. He fpoke no *German*, and the King fpoke no *Englifh*; confequently, it was through a rudimentary *Latin*, that they had communicated their Wifhes and Defigns to one another.

After the firft *King George* departed from this Life, Matters of State became a little eafier for the Man who was now ſtyled *Sir Robert*, for his Majeſty *King George II* knew a little of the *Engliſh* Tongue; as too did his noble Spouſe the late *Queen Caroline*, who was bleſſed with a Surfeit of Intellect and Genius, that ſurely ſhe might have been capable as a Ruler on her own Part, had the Forces of Deſtiny not rendered her being of the Female Sex. A cloſe, and perhaps even fond Partnerſhip, was eſtabliſhed between *Sir Robert* and the Queen. Whenſoever it tranſpired that he could not perſuade the King to act as he thought was beſt, he could perſuade the Queen inſtead, who would ſee to it that her Husband, ſoon thereafter, came into Agreement with her. This Arrangement was nearly common Knowledge acroſs the Kingdom, and had been the Subject of many humorous Plays and Farces.

Indeed, the Theatre had never ſhrunk at any Opportunity to lampoon the Anticks of the Politicians. *England* did not inhibit its Theatre in the way that ſome leſs civiliſed Nations had found fit to do. For moſt of a Century there had been no Trouble at all with this Arrangement, untill it fell that too much Power became concentrated in the Hands of one Man, thoſe being the grimey Trotters of the so-call'd Prime Miniſter.

The Trouble had commenced with that famous Compoſition by Mr. *John Gay*, call'd *The Beggar's Opera,* which is celebrated through all the *Engliſh*-ſpeaking World. One finds the Action of the Play to ſurround the cunning Highwayman

Macheath, who, as any one who has ſeen this Entertainment can atteſt, is a plain *caricature* of *Sir Robert*. All the *dialogue* of *Macheath* making Bribes to Officials, and of robbing thoſe he does not bribe, are plainly Jokes at *Sir Robert*'s expenſe. *Macheath's* inſtinct for *polygamy* is alſo a Laugh at *Sir Robert*, who was known by the Publick to have both his Wife and his Miſtreſs, at that Time. *Sir Robert* felt that, at this Jeſt, the Theatre had finally taken Matters far enough; and from thenceforth he watch'd with Hawkiſh Eyes that they would not proceed farther. He did what he could againſt Mr. *Gay*, by ſeeking to ſuppreſs his next Play, which was a Sequel to *The Beggar's Opera* intitled *Polly; or, Macheath Turn'd Pyrate*. *Sir Robert* achieved this End by a Bribe to the Theatre's Manager, who, in conſideration of the Sum, felt a ſudden pang of Conſcience, and would not permit so vile a Spectacle to be ſtaged. The Scandal only enhanc'd the Demand for the ſhew of it; yet even for a Man of *Sir Robert's* brilliant Capacity, there was no lawful way to retaliate againſt *John Gay*, for the Play had not overtly named any one in a manner that would permit a Criminal Charge of Libel. Poor Mr. *Gay* enjoyed his Succeſs whilſt he could, but he ſoon afterwards died, of cauſes unrelated to *Macheath* or to *Sir Robert*.

One might have thought *Sir Robert* would be appeas'd at this, for the Culprit was gone and would never return; however, tho' the Author was no more, the mad Succeſs of his Play had ſpawned a Horde of eager Imitators. Soon enough, every Performance upon the Stage was a Lampoon of *Engliſh* politicks; and, like feral Cats ſet looſe in a Creamery, the Audiences lapp'd it with Zeal.

The final Inſult had been rendered by that moſt notorious Farce, the indeſcribably cutting *Paſquin,* by Mr. *Henry Fielding*. This ſaid Farce, had made a Tilt at *Engliſh* Politicks and Politicians, in a manner more bold-fac'd than ever before was conceived — and what was there to be done about it, by *Sir Robert*, the King, and every elſe who was made Butte of its Satire? There was Nothing at all; for not only had *Fielding* wiſely conſtructed his Farce as a Play within a Play, which befitted to him the Excuſe, that he did not ridicule Politicians, but rather that he ridiculed thoſe Men who wrote ſuch Ridicules; but in addition to this, he was alſo protected by that ſame Peculiarity of *Engliſh* Law, which had protected Mr. *Gay*: that is to ſay, that altho' all Entertainments were *intended* to be examin'd and approved by the *Lord Chamberlain* before they ſhould be perform'd upon the Stage, this Action was rarely ever taken by the Managers of Theatres, the Reaſon being that there was no Penalty of Law for a Failure to ſeek the *Lord Chamberlain's* Approval. With that being the Caſe, why ſhould one be bother'd to pay his Fee to read the Manuſcript at all? Only if a future Difficulty or Diſturbance were firſt anticipated, was it ever done.

It thereby came that any vile, or offenſive Thing at all, could be played, provided the Proprietor of the Theatre had adequate comfort with putting it up on his own Stage, where it was to be enacted alongſide the mighty Nobles who took their Seats there with the Actors — for they could Hoot and Hiſs like any others, and could make a Failure, in the Publick's Eye, if they did not approve.

As far as the Law was applicable, the ſtrongeſt criminal Charge that could be made againſt an offenſive Performance of a Play, was that of Libel — and it was not the Playwrights nor the Managers of the Theatre who took the Puniſhment in thoſe Caſes, but the Actors (ſince it was, inevitably, the Actors who had *ſaid* the Words.) It was a uſeleſs Law — yet *Sir Robert* ſtill found means to turn it to ſome Advantage for himſelf, for he us'd it to bring under his Power an Actor and Theatre Manager, of middle Age, by the Name of *Henry Giffard*. Poor *Giffard* had committed the Errour of playing a Role in a certain Entertainment, intitled *Harlequin Shipwreck'd, or; King Oberon*. Now, had the *Fairy King Oberon* been made an Emperor, a Mogul, or even a Length of Sauſages, all ſhould have been well for this Man; but inſtead *Oberon* was a King, and so the Company, it was ſaid, had inſulted *The King of England*, by ſpeaking the Lines of the Farce. In order that he ſhould avoid a criminal Charge of Libel for himſelf, and that he ſhould protect the reſt of the Company from the ſame, poor Mr. *Giffard* was forced to aſſiſt *Sir Robert,* in the Name of ſome new-hatched Scheme, concocted by the latter of them, which was meant to remedy the exceſſive Freedoms which were then enjoyed by the modern *Britiſh* Theatre.

It now behooves me to confeſs that I am that ſame Mr. *Giffard* who had so been enſlaved by the Miniſter. My Reaſons for writing this Account of my Time with *Sir Robert* ſhall be, I believe, made apparent by the Finiſh of this Work; tho' if they be not made plain enough, then I ſhall here ſay it plainly: *I wiſh to ſhame a Man who deſerves to be aſhamed of his Conduct.*

He had compelled me to go to his Houſe in *London*, that property on *Downing Street* known as *The Houſe At The Back*. I was ſummon'd in the Morning, and he did not permit me to leave all Day, but put me at a Deſk with a Quire of Paper, a Quill, Ink, Knives, and commanding me to write for him a Play which, *per* his Specifications, muſt be of the utmoſt offenſive and ridiculous Nature.

"Why, particularly, muſt I author this "Play?" I aſked of him. "I am no Playwright. I "only act and ſtage what Others have compoſed." — "It does not matter," anſwered *Sir Robert*. "The Play needn't be good. Indeed, that is the "Oppoſite to what I ſhould wiſh. It muſt be ſure to "give Offenſe, to inſpire Hatred and Diſguſt in all "who read it, and that is all."

"Be that so, then why do not you write it, "your own ſelf?" aſked I. "You ſeem to know the "Details of your Needs, certainly better than I ever "ſhall." — "I am a buſy man, Mr. *Giffard,*" anſwered *Sir Robert.* "I have so much Work to do, "already, on the *Scottiſh* matter; and do not doubt, "it's no eaſy Taſk to puniſh the *Scots* for that "*Porteous Riot,* without offending all the *Scotchmen* "in Parliament, who take a legitimate Puniſhment "for a Crime againſt *Engliſh* rule, to be ſome "Affront againſt their Race. Now, I have so many "Plans to make, many Meſſages to write, and to "ſend — so you ſhall do as you are taſk'd, and "ſimply write the Play I have requeſted."

I fell ſilent. As could I thus toſs away my Care, I ſhrugged my Shoulders, and finding no Gratification by my Endeavor, I took up the Quill that had been provided for me. I was commanded to write a Play, and it was unneceſſary that it ſhould be good; it could fairly be ſaid, that it was ſimple enough of a Taſk, that any Perſon who could write at all could make a Succeſs of it.

"What ſhall be the Title?" aſked I. — "Any Thing you pleaſe," replied *Sir Robert,* perturbed. "Juſt be ſure that it ſounds like the Name "of a Play, and that it be outrageous. It needn't be "any *Drury-Lane* degree of Wit — *Southwark* or "*Bartholomew* Fair will do."

I gave ſome Contemplation to what might ſate his Demands, and of a ſudden I recalled a Cartoon, which I had obſerved ſome weeks before at the Print-Shop Window, intitled *The Feſtival of The Golden Rump*. This Cartoon was an obvious Joke of the King, Queen, and Miniſtry, featuring a deviliſh Idol whoſe Fundament was worſhipped. It ſufficed for my Inſpiration. Without Care, I wrote the name *The Golden Rump* acroſs the top Sheet and began to conſider, next, what ſhould be the Plot of this Farce.

"Mr. *Giffard*, I hear not the ſcraping of "your Pen," ſaid *Sir Robert* from acroſs the Room. He ſpoke in a ſcolding Tone, without looking upward from the Papers he wrote out on his own Part. I made the Excuſe to him that I was thinking. "Think leſs, write more," he replied. "The Houſe "might begin to debate upon the *Licenſing Act* any "Day now, and I muſt have the Manuſcript to "preſent to them, when they ſhall."

In reply I aſked, why did he not merely bring in the ready Text of *Charles I* or *Paſquin*, for both theſe Plays had been very bad, and indeed had provided the Motivation for his Operation — "Becauſe they were performed and applauded," he replied. "They will ſay that their Content is fair, "ſince it did not cauſe much Offenſe except to thoſe "who, rightly, ought to have been ſhamed by it. I "muſt have a Play so unabaſhedly inſulting that "Nobody, not even a Whig, would abide it."

"But you ſay it is not to be performed?" I aſk'd. — "Quite right," ſaid he. "I only need to "read Paſſages aloud to the Houſe, and tell them "that you gave me this Play becauſe ſome one had "wiſh'd to perform it. If the Play is offenſive, as it "ought to be, they ſhall be appalled that ſome one "intended to ſtage ſuch Material, and they will "favour my Side in ſuppreſſing the Manuſcripts "*before* they can go to the Stage." — To which I aſk'd, "Then why do you not but bribe every one to "vote as you pleaſe, as is your accuſtomary "Proviſion?" — "Damn it, *Giffard*! My Pockets are "not so deep that I can ſimply bribe every body; to "make no mention of the Fact, that a few honeſt "Men do remain, who like Devils ſhall refuſe to be "bribed." At this I began to laugh, untill I recogniſed that he did not jeſt. He ſpoke on: — "To paſs this Bill, I muſt have Support all around "— and that includes *Pultney* and *Cheſterfield*, the "Prince of *Wales*, *Boilingbroke* and every body. So: "write a Play that features all of 'em (in plain "*caricature*, of courſe) as they accept bribes, and "look ridiculous. Is that ſimple enough for even a "Simpleton like you?" — "Yes, Sir, to be ſure," I replied ſoftly, feeling the Smart of his deliberate Wound, but knowing little that could amend for it.

I began to write the beſt Joke I could think of: —

Act 1. Scene 1. Enter PESTERFIELD *and* POXNEY, *coming from a Brothel.*

At that very Moment a male Servant entered into the Chamber bearing a Baſket of Apples, the which he ſet down before *Sir Robert.* His Maſter acknowledged him, and in the ſame Breath diſmiſſed him. *Sir Robert* began, then, to eat the Apples very greedfully, whilſt poring over his Papers. This notorious Habit of always ſuſtaining himſelf upon Apples, doubtleſs contributed to his enormous Weight. In the meantime, I ſtarved; for *Sir Robert* offered me Nothing, deſpite having kept me all the Day. Me thus ſuppoſing that Occupation would prove itſelf a happy Diſtraction for my diſcomfort, I ſtruggled paſt the inviſible Barrier which withheld my Pen, by thinking on *Paſquin.* Its Satire was celebrated, or damned, depending which Side you were of. I tried to recollect its Story, and recall'd, that it had been ſome thing about two different Plays, one a Tragedy of *Queen Common-Senſe* and *Queen Ignorance,* the two noble Ladies being manipulated by a Prieſt of the Sun, called *Firebrand;* the other Play within the Play had been a Comedy, in which one *Lord Place* and *Colonel Promiſe,* bribed the Inhabitants of a ſmall Village to vote them into Office. In Reality, it was little more than mere Enactments of the current political Scandals, veiled so thinly that it was leſs a Veil than a broken Window to peer into. I reaſſured myſelf, that it would be of little Difficulty to write ſomething so artleſs as all that. I then conſidered what had been the biggeſt Scandal of the Year, and without too much thought, I dropp'd upon the late Diſappearance of the King; for tho' he is King of *Great Britain*, he is alſo the King of *Hannover*, in *Germany*, which directs that he ſhould travel thither and thence from Time to Time, and at a Rate that many *Britons* reſent as nearing exceſſive. It was during the Winter previous to theſe told Events, that his Majeſty had made juſt ſuch a Voyage (againſt the Advice of his Miniſters) which cauſed him to be, a while, loſt at Sea in bad Weather. For this, there was great Alarm and Concern throughout the Land, as can be ſuppoſed; and that was worſened when he was abſent from the opening of Parliament. There came to be much Dread amongſt the Tories that *Frederick*, Prince of *Wales* (a definite Whig, and who puts out little to maſk the Diſcord between himſelf and his Parents) ſhould ſoon be crowned. It took ſeveral Weeks before the Storms were ſoftened to a Degree which permitted any Ships to croſs the Sea, but when at laſt it did, Word was finally received in *England* that the King was ſafe and ſound; he had been caught in the Storm, to be ſure — but he had returned to *Germany* and waited there, in comfort, untill fairer Weather was come on. When I recalled this to Mind, I perceived a great potential for a ſhew to be made from it, and thus I began to write a merry Tale of a poor Link-Boy taken into the Palace of a ſuppoſed foreign Country, where he often ſaid the Phraſe "I Serve" which, I hoped, the Audience ſhould recogniſe as a Reference to the Prince of *Wales's* motto *Ich Dien*, and thus would perceive that the Link-Boy repreſented the Prince of *Wales*. This ſeemed to me an ideal Inſult, for not only did that place the Prince of *Wales* as the Hero of the Spectacle, to affront the King; but alſo, to be depicted as a Link-Boy, was ſure to offend even the Prince of *Wales*.

I had not written long when I became aware of a gigantine, Human-ſcented Preſence which hovered above my very Shoulders, and I call'd up to him, "*Sir Robert*, if you pleaſe, you ſee that I "do work on it. I have no need of an Overſeer."

"You muſt mention the *South-Sea Bubble*," ſaid *Sir Robert*, *a propos* of Nothing.

"With Submiſſion," I anſwered, "Nobody "cares about that old Stock Scheme, *Sir Robert*. It "was near twenty Years ago. Any body who loſt "their Money in conſequence of that, has ſurely "made it back by now — through receiving your "Bribes."

Sir Robert laughed heartily at that; and I did feel ſome Conſolation in that I was falling upon the proper Path. He then replied to me: "Men, and "eſpecially Noblemen, of a certain age are ſtill "enrag'd if one but mentions the Phraſe, *South-Sea* "*Bubble*. Put it in, ſomehow." — "I ſhall ſee what

"I can do," I ſaid. "But leave me be, if you will "have this done ſwiftly. I don't write any faſter for "having ſome one ſtooped over my Back."

"Like a Bardiſh?" aſked *Sir Robert*, laughing at his own vile Joke.

"You are diſguſting!" cried I, for I was confounded by the very ſuggeſtion of Sodomy, which was not only made in so Caſual a Manner as to ſuggeſt it had been already upon his Mind, but which was too ſevere for me to Stomach in general. To inſult Politicians was no great Immorality, in my View, but it was ſomething elſe to inſult the *Almighty*. *Sir Robert* did not ſeem to be moved by my Diſtreſs, and he returned to his Chair, laughing and eating an Apple, in a manner that left me deadly amaz'd that the Man did not choke upon it.

Barely was I reſumed of my writing, when *Sir Robert* cut up afreſh: — "Alſo, there ought to "be an Elephant in it." — "An Elephant?" aſked I. "Why do you ſay this?" — "It is a little Joke I "have with ſome body I know." — "Well! Then, "is that what you wiſh? I had underſtood that the "very Purpoſe for my writing this Piece, was to "diſguiſe your Involvement." — "A little Joke ſuch "as that will not be too obvious. Juſt jot it in, "ſomewhere." — "Would you ſooner that I take "Dictation from you, *Sir Robert*, ſince you have so "many fine Ideas?"

He had marked the tartneſs of my Tone, and reſponded to it with: "You lazy Cod! I ſhould "not have to do all the Work for you, would you "haſten to do it, yourſelf."

"I tell you," ſaid I, "I make faſter Work "when I'm without Interruption. Why not have me "labour upon this at mine own Houſe? It ſhall "proceed much faſter there, I'm ſure of it." — "To "your Houſe, and have your Wife diſcover it, and "ſhe ſpill the News that you were its Author, to "every body?" replied *Sir Robert* with a Tone of Miſchief. "Why, that would ſimply add to your "Charge of Libel."

At this I groaned, feeling my Enſlavement too ſharply.

It was at this that *Sir Robert's* Servant again entered the Room, now bearing with him a Letter. "May it pleaſe your Honour," ſaid he, "you have a "Meſſage from the Queen."

My Ears were prick'd up by thoſe Words. The very Queen, her Majeſty herſelf, had ſent a Meſſage to this Houſe! To a Man of my Poſition, to be in the Preſence of ſuch great Tidings, was mortal exciting News. I wondered what it might have been about. On the other Hand, the Miniſter did not ſeem much ſtirr'd by the Event. "O, what's that fat "Bitch want now?" groaned he, as he took the Letter and unſealed it. I obſerved him read, and I perceived that his Countenance altered, from one of utmoſt Indifference, to one of Alarm.

"*Giffard*, ceaſe what you're about," ſaid he, whilſt ariſing from his Seat and dropping the Letter upon the Floor. "Come with me, immediately. We "muſt haſten to the Theatre in time for to-night's "Performance." — "Which Theatre?" aſk'd I, taken quite by Surpriſe. "Surely not mine?" — "No, not to yours," ſaid *Sir Robert*, now towſing me by my Coat. "The *New Theatre* in "the *Hay-Market.*"

At that I knew what we were to ſee. "That's Mr. *Fielding's* ſhew! *The Hiſtorical Regiſter* "*for 1736.*" — "Indeed," ſaid *Sir Robert*. "He has, "evidently, appended ſomething new to it, and the "Queen believes I ought have a Look. This "concerns you alſo, therefore, hurry up yourſelf and "wait me."

As I was given no Option to do otherwiſe, I was pull'd along by *Sir Robert*, and together we rode in the Miniſter's Coach to the *Hay-Market*.

"You'd beſt ſtoop down as we ride; I "ſhouldn't wiſh to be ſeen with you," ſaid *Sir Robert*.

"Then why bring me out at all?" I objected, tho' proſtrating myſelf the ſame.

"Becauſe this concerns you, and your Taſk. "Our Friend, Mr. *Fielding*, has compoſed a new "Play." When I objected that *The Hiſtorical Regiſter* had been running for many Days previous, I was anſwered: "It has — and a perfectly "objectionable Piece it is — but there is a new "After-Piece appended, and her Majeſty "recommends that I ſhou'd watch it, and not "becauſe ſhe thinks I'll enjoy it."

"Then how are we both to ſee it, if we "cannot be ſeen together?" I aſk'd. — "We ſhall "not," ſaid he. "You ſhall watch it for me. I have "other Buſineſs to overtake. Simply go within, "purchaſe what ever your uſual Seat ſhould be — "I'll compenſate you, if you require it — and you "give Attention to the Performance and to what it is "they ſay. Afterwards, return to my Houſe and "await me, if I'm not diſcover'd back at Home "already."

I was releaſed into a Back-Alley, away from the Theatre, to which I walked by myſelf, thro' filth-ſlick'd Streets. It was early in the Evening, and the City's new Lamps were not yet alight on *Hay-Market*. It was rather *too* early, indeed, for moſt Men to arrive for the Play-Houſe, but for a Man as myſelf — Proprietor of the Theatre at *Goodman's-Fields*, and a proficient Actor to boot — it was not unreaſonable, unſeaſonable, nor ſuſpicious, to arrive so early, for it could be ſuppos'd that I ſhould ſpend ſome While with fellow *Theſpians*. I had, moreover, been very hungry when leaving *The Houſe At The Back*, and I had imagined I might firſt look into a Pie-Shop or a Tavern, before proceeding to the Theatre; but the ſheer Quantity of *London* Filth that Night, was enough to murder my Appetite, and I ſimply went forward to the Theatre. To ſtep in

Shit from Horſe, Dog, Pig, or Man, was a known Hazard to thoſe who walk'd in this Part of the City. The Play-House was no better; the Wind of the Place was noticeable as one advanc'd upon it, for it was the habit of all Patrons, and Actors too, to piſs on the outſide Walls during the Intervals, and whenſoever elſe the Need aroſe. One entered the *New-Theatre Hay-Market* welcomed by this harſh, Ammoniacal Perfume which would have done well for a Lady's ſmelling Salt. (Not as my very clean Theatre in *Goodman's-Fields,* which in compariſon, is neſtled in a Situation nearly paſtoral, with freſh, green Herbs all around it, which render the Building very comfortable for all its Patrons; and thoſe who are of the complaint that "It is too far" ſhall find their ſmall inconvenience very chearfully rewarded when they come to *Goodman's-Fields* and ſee what Benefit the freſh Air and modeſt Population make toward the enjoyment of the Performances, which are enacted by Players who are all excelled in the Art.)

I paſſed ſome Time with the *Hay-Market* Players in the Green-Room, myſelf making a concerted Effort, all the While, not to ſay any Thing about the Performance to come, for Fear that I might prove too much tempted, to warn my Friends about the true Purpoſe behind my Attendance on that Evening. As the riſe of the Curtain approached, Mr. *Lacy,* with his Face already painted up, ſaw me to the Pit, where I was to have my Seat.

"May you enjoy the ſhew," ſaid *Lacy*.

"I've heard it is very naughty," ſaid I, only now daring to hint at Foreknowledge of the Play.

"No more than the Politicians," replied *Lacy*, and he hurried away to dreſs himſelf in his Coſtume.

At laſt the Theatre was filled. The Nobles were ſtation'd upon the Stage where they could be well ſeen in their Finery, and the Curtain roſe upon the firſt Spectacle of the Night: *The Hiſtorical Regiſter for 1736*. This was faſhion'd after the accuſtomary Manner that Mr. *Henry Fielding* had lately employed for his Satire, which conſiſted of depicting Theatre People who ſtaged a Play, in which the Play within the Play really contaiued all of the political Commentary. It was a moſt clever way to protect himſelf, and his Actors, from complaints about the Satire. In the opening Scene, one of the Players declar'd his Vexation that, in this new Play, the Jeers were not ſtrong enough:—

"I would have a humming Deal of Satire, "and I would repeat it in every Page, that Courtiers "are Cheats and don't pay their Debts, that Lawyers "are Rogues, Phyſicians Block-Heads, Soldiers "Cowards, and Miniſters ..." Here he fell ſilent.

"What what, Sir?" aſked the ſecond Player.

"Nay, I'll only name 'em, that's enough to "ſet the Audience a-hooting."

The veritable Audience laughed at the Joke of the Actor-Actor, and ſoon the remaining Players were all about in ſinging a merry *Ode to the New Year* and beginning their ſhew, which was ſuppoſed to be ſet in the notorious political Quandary of *Corſica*, wherein, at that Time, a Revolution was, in real Life, about. On the Stage was diſcover'd a mute Fellow, who bore ſuch a ſtunning reſemblance to *Sir Robert*, that any one who had ever ſeen the Man, or even a Portrait of him, couldn't fail in the Recognition. The other Actors playing Politicians bumbled laughably, and talked of raiſing up Taxes for an Aſſortment of ludicrous Purpoſes. It was all plainly a political Jeſt — but Nothing worſe than was regularly ſaid in the News-Papers each Day. When the Politicians were gone, the Character of the Playwright declar'd:

"And this, Sir, is the full Account of the "Hiſtory of *Europe*, as far as we know it, in one "Scene." And the Audience howled with Laughter.

The next Scene had its Place in *London*, and it made ridicule of female Politicians, who fretted over their Appearances, and fawned over the Singer *Farinelli*, more than they truly took Concern with any ſerious Politicks. It was ſurely a Jeſt at the Queen and the Princeſſes, but Nothing overt enough nor, arguably, falſe enough to claim Treaſonous. Thə Scene of the Ladies continued into a fantaſtick

Interlude of an Auction for Items ſuch as "three "Grains of Modeſty" and "a very clear Conſcience "which has been worn by a Judge" which was very amuſing.

It was in the Third Act where the Satire became moſt bold-faced. After ſome reference to *The Beggar's Opera,* that invoked its well-known Jeſts at *Sir Robert*, out came Players who repreſented the baſtard Son of *Apollo,* and ſeveral ſhabby Patriots.

"Proſperity to *Corſica!*" — "Liberty and Proſperity!" — "Succeſs to Trade!" they cried.

"Ay, to Trade, to Trade — particularly to "my Shop," cried the laſt, hitching up his Breeches in a Manner that all recogniſed as a Ridicule of *Sir Robert's* Brother, *Horatio Walpole.*

Then the Falſe *Sir Robert* appeared on Stage a ſecond Time, as a Character named *Quidam* (Ha! Ha!) who brought forth a Purſe of Money to fund *Corſica's* War, and following so, began to play Tunes on a Fiddle, whilſt they all danced away. Two of the Characters explained: "Every one of theſe "Patriots have a Hole in their Pockets, as Mr. "*Quidam* the Fiddler there knows, so that he intends "to make them dance till all the Money is fallen "through, which he will pick up again, and so not "loſe one Half-Penny by his Generoſity." And at a cloſing *monologue* the Curtain fell, to great Applauſe. I clapp'd with the Reſt of 'em; the Actors were not the Beſt I've ſeen, but the Text was written ſmartly enough to accommodate their

Talents. The entirety of the ſhew was clearly made for the mere purpoſe of giving Inſult to Politicians, but it was Nothing too heinous — and Nothing new to the Stage, to be ſure. However, it was not this Performance, but the ſecond upon the Play-Bill, that had alarmed *Sir Robert*, and after an Interval, it was on: the one call'd *Eurydice Hiſſ'd.*

It was a Reformation of a Play that was intitled *Eurydice; or, the Devil Henpeck'd,* which had been so materially offenſive, that it had been played for only one Night at *Drury-Lane* before it was hiſs'd from the Stage whilſt inciting a Riot. How much of its origin remained part of the Reworking, I did not know, for I had not ſeen its principal Run. Three Actors came upon the Stage, theſe being the Perſons of *Spatter, Sowrwit* and *Lord Dapper.*

"My Lord," ſaid *Spatter.* "I am extremely "obliged to you for the Honour you ſhew me in "ſtaying to the Rehearſal of my Tragedy: I hope it "will pleaſe your Lordſhip, as well as Mr. *Medley's* "Comedy has, for I aſſure you it's ten Times as "ridiculous."

"Is it the Merit of a Tragedy, Mr. *Spatter*, "to be ridiculous?" aſked *Sowrwit.*

"Yes, Sir, of ſuch Tragedies as mine; and I "think you, Mr. *Sowrwit*, will grant me this, that a "Tragedy had better be ridiculous than dull; and "that there is more Merit in making the Audience "laugh, than in ſetting them aſleep."

What commenced from there was a Work of Genius, of Talent, of the utmoſt Ability; and all notwithſtanding the limited Talents of the *Hay-Market's* Company of Actors. (Not like the very reſpectable Company you ſhall obſerve at *Goodman's-Fields*, which have been ſelected for their Talent and have received, moreover, Inſtruction in the Art of Acting from two very well-known Perſons; and the Theatre being of a very ſnug and compact Size, there is no Difficulty to be encountered, in obſerving or in hearing their moſt laudable Performances.) The entire Performance of *Eurydice Hiſſ'd* was a maſſive *double-entendre*, where Mr. *Fielding* had contrived a Character, *Pillage*, who was an obvious Parody of himſelf, but alſo of *Sir Robert Walpole*. This meant that, altho' the Inſults to *Sir Robert* were clear to every body, *Fielding* could merely ſay, to his Defenſe, that he had criticiſed and ridiculed no perſon but himſelf; and ſhould the Prime Miniſter perceive any of it to apply to *him* — well, he may wear the Cap if it fits.

"Well, Sir," demanded *Sowrwit*, at a Scene of *Pillage* at his morning *levee*. "And pray what do "you principally intend by this *levee* Scene?"

"Sir," anſwered *Spatter*, "I intend firſt to "warn all future Authors from depending ſolely on a "Party to ſupport them againſt the Judgment of the "Town. Secondly, ſhewing that even the Author of a "Farce may have his Attendants and Dependants; I "hope greater Perſons may learn to deſpiſe them, "which may be a more uſeful Moral than you may "apprehend; for perhaps the mean Ambition of "being worſhipp'd, flatter'd and attended by ſuch "Fellows as theſe, may have led Men into the worſt "of Schemes, from which they could promiſe "themſelves little more."

Then onto the Stage came *Honeſtus*, a Parody of *William Shippen* who, in Jokes, was known as the only honeſt Man in Parliament; and the Players ſpoke of both the Play-Houſe and the Houſe of Parliament.

Said *Pillage*:— "My Farce appears this "Day upon the Stage, and I intreat your preſence in "the Pit, to help applaud it." — "Faith, Sir," replied *Honeſtus*, "my Voice ſhall never be corrupt. "If I approve your Farce, I will applaud it; if not, "I'll hiſs it, tho' I hiſs alone."

"Now, by my Soul," retorted *Pillage*, "I "hope to ſee the Time when none ſhall dare to hiſs "within the Houſe." — "I rather hope to ſee the "Time, when none ſhall come prepar'd to cenſure or "applaud, but Merit always bear away the Prize. If "you have Merit, take your Merit's due; if not, why "ſhould a Bungler in his Art, keep off ſome better "Genius from the Stage? I tell you, Sir, the Farce "you act to-night, I don't approve, nor will the "Houſe, unleſs your Friends by Partiality prevail." — "I fear them not," ſaid *Pillage*, "I have so "many Friends, that the Majority will ſure be "mine." — "Curſe on this way of carrying Things "by Friends! This Bar to Merit, by ſuch unjuſt "Means, a Play's Succeſs or Ill-Succeſs is known, "and fix'd, before it has been try'd i'th' Houſe; "When Friends are not, and the impartial Judge "ſhall with the meaneſt Scribbler rank your Name, "who would not rather wiſh a *Butler's* fame, "diſtreſſ'd, and poor in every Thing but Merit, than "be the blundering Laureat to a Court?"

"Not I! On me," ſaid *Pillage*, "ye Gods, "beſtow the Pence, and give your Fame to any Fools "you pleaſe."

"Your love of Pence," ſaid *Honeſtus*, "ſufficiently you ſhew, by raiſing ſtill your Prices on "the Town." — "The Town for their own Sakes "thoſe Prices pay, which the additional Expenſe "demands."

When *Pillage* was at laſt diſappointed by the Refuſal of *Honeſtus*, his *Muſe* came to viſit him. She was clothed exactly alike to a Portrait of the Queen.

"Why wears my gentle *Muſe* so ſtern a "Brow?" aſked *Pillage*, opening his Arms to her. "Why, awful thus affects ſhe to appear, where ſhe "delighted to be so ſerene?" — "And doſt thou "aſk," replied the *Muſe*, "thou Traitor, doſt thou "aſk? Art thou not conſcious of the Wrongs I bear, "neglected, ſlighted for a freſher *Muſe*? I, whoſe "fond Heart too eaſily did yield my virgin Joys and "Honour to thy Arms, and bore thee *Paſquin*?"

At this I ſigh'd and groaned, knowing fully this was the ſort of Thing *Sir Robert* was moſt diſquieted for. "*But ſurely it is natural that the Muſe* "*ſhould look like a Queen to an Author,*" so *Fielding* would argue; and if it ſuggeſted any Thing of Conduct between the Queen and ſome Perſon, well, that was ſome one elſe who ſaid it, not *Fielding*, and to be ſure not any of the Players who ſaid it.

Later, *Pillage's* play of *Eurydice* was to be ſtaged. "But don't you intend to lay the Scene in the "Theatre, and let us ſee the Farce fairly damn'd "before us?" aſked *Sourwit*.

Spatter anſwer'd rapidly, "No, Sir, it is a "Thing of too horrible a Nature; for which Reaſon, "I ſhall follow *Horace's* Rule, and only introduce a "Deſcription of it. Come, enter, Deſcription; I "aſſure you I have thrown myſelf out greatly in this "next Scene."

Enter Gentleman 3. "O, Friends, all's loſt; "*Eurydice* is damn'd!" — "Ha! Damn'd?" aſked Gentleman 2. "A few ſhort Moments paſt I came "from the Pit-Door, and heard a loud Applauſe." — "'Tis true," replied 3, "at firſt the Pit ſeem'd "greatly pleas'd, and loud Applauſes thro' the "Benches rung, but as the Plot began to open more "— a ſhallow Plot — the Claps leſs frequent grew, "till by Degrees a gentle Hiſs aroſe; this by a "Cat-Call from the Gallery was quickly "ſeconded: then follow'd Claps, and long 'twixt "Claps and Hiſſes, did ſucceed a ſtern Contention:

"Victory hung dubious. So hangs the Confcience, "doubtful to determine, when Honefty pleads here "and there a Bribe. At length, from fome ill-fated "Actor's mouth, fudden there iffued forth a horrid "Dram, and from another rufh'd two Gallons forth: "the Audience, as it were contagious Air, all caught "it, holloo'd, cat-call'd, hifs'd, and groan'd."

Refponding to the Failure of his Play, forth came *Pillage*, drinking Gin from out a hollow'd Apple, as if it were a Cup, and making a drunken Stagger about the Stage.

"O! It is now too late. Already I have "drank two Bottles off, of this fell Potion, and it "now begins to work its deadly Purpofe on my "Brain." He then fwooned drunk to the Floor-Boards, leaving *Honeftus* to ftate the Conclufion whilft ftanding over him, and at this at laft the Curtain fell.

When *Sir Robert* learned, from me, what Crimes had tranfpired upon the *Hay-Market's* Stage, he was not taken by fhock, for he had expected Nothing more from it.

"How would you fay it compares, to your "*Harlequin Shipwreck'd*?" afked he, naming the accurs'd Play for which I had facrificed my Freedom.

"I think it far worſe," anſwer'd I to the Miniſter, not advancing that our Play had contained no Satire whatſoever, and it was but the exceſſive Senſitivities of the People that had put forth that the Shipwreck meant we wiſh'd the King ſhipwreck'd in *Germany*. *Sir Robert*, for his part, nodded aſſent to my Words.

"This is the very Reaſon," ſaid he, "why "we muſt paſs this Act. The Playwrights will only "increaſe their Satire, and their Means of veiling it, "and they won't be ſatisfied till a Riot is bred in the "Pit at every Performance. They have already tried "to murder the King, once, at the Theatre — we "cannot permit that it happen again!"

Indeed, ſome Years ago, when his Majeſty *George II* ſtill was Prince of *Wales*, ſome Jacobite had tried to kill him as he watched a Farce, at *Drury-Lane*; and tho' it was without probability that the Farce on the Stage had at all influenced the Plan of this would-be Aſſaſſin, the Miniſter's Point was well underſtood by me. "I ſhall do my beſt to write the "Satire in the ſame ſtyle," ſaid I.

"Do no ſuch Thing. That was too tame, "for it was fit to be ſtaged at all," replied *Sir Robert*. "We muſt ſtart afreſh — burn all you've "written. We muſt create a Play so *filthy* no Man "would ever permit it viewed. It muſt be "unſtageable, inſulting to All and Sundry, abſent of "any Merit whatſoever."

"But then, who would believe that ſome "one try'd to ſtage it?" aſked I. — "You are the "Witneſs to that, for you ſhall ſimply ſay as much. "That is why you ſhall have the Manuſcript in your "poſſeſſion, becauſe (you ſhall declare) ſome one "came to you, wiſhing it ſtaged at your Theatre; but "it gave ſuch Offenſe to read, that you reported it to "me, for Fear of its Power."

"Be that so, if we are to burn what was "already compoſed; we have then Nothing but a "Title, *The Golden Rump.*" — "The Title will "ſerve," ſaid *Sir Robert.* "And your Story of the "Prince of *Wales* as a Hero in the Palace will "ſuffice. It is the Events that muſt be rendered "harſher." — "Well what, then? What can make "*The Golden Rump* become more heinous? Shall we "dreſs the Stage in naked Rumps?" — "That will "do well," anſwered *Sir Robert,* and he began to write out the Stage Directions himſelf:

Setting is a Temple within a royal Palace, in the figure of a great Buttocks, the Door which is the Entrance to the Stage being the ſphincter ani. Courtiers, Magician *and* Ganymede *enter together.* Ganymede *hath Pencil and a Note-Book.*

The name of the Character was new; I had called him *Proſpect* in my verſion. "Why "*Ganymede*?" aſked I.

"If I ſay it is from *Shakeſpere*, will that be "veiled enough for you?" aſked *Sir Robert* with his Eye-Brow up.

I told him I did not yet comprehend his Meaning. He finally anſwered: "It is a very "*ſynonymon* for a He-Whore amongſt the Sodomites "in this City."

At this I was aghaſt. "You don't dare —" — "I dare all. Every Thing has to be dared. The "King ſhould be more afraid of what's on Stage, "than of his Piles ... O!" He haſtily wrote out another Stage Direction, and I went white, as I conſidered what it ſhould lead to.

"Egads, do you mean you ſhall laugh at the "King's Piles?" aſked I. — "Doesn't every one but "he?" ſaid *Sir Robert*. — "And is the Queen to be "ſpared any Thing?" aſked I. — "We ſhall ſet half "the Play in a Gaol. You know how ſhe loves the "Gaols. Charity to Priſoners is her favourite cauſe, "apart from the ſponſorſhip of mawkiſh Poetry."

"Yet, I ſhould not think that remarking her "Charity to Priſoners, be ſomething for her to feel "an Inſult by," ſaid I. — "Juſt you wait and ſee," anſwered he.

It was now *Sir Robert* about moſt of the writing, myſelf ſerving only as a Retort for his Ideas. And ſuch Ideas *Sir Robert* had! The wicked Things he conjured forth and wrote upon the Paper ſhould have provok'd a bluſh from even the antient Emperor *Caligula*. For the Miniſter's Purpoſe, to infult only Politicians was inadequate; to render his Point, he did not hefitate to infult Men, Women, himfelf, his Friends, Nature, and the *Almighty*. I was fully appalled, that a Man I had talked to, and affociated with, could have fuch foul Maggots bouncing within his Head. And yet, at Times his Store of them ran thin, for there were Occafions at which I obferved him to borrow from known Comedies.

"Is this Scene not very fimilar to one that "was in *The Beggar's Opera*?" I would afk. — "Blaft it, it does not matter. *Gay* was allow'd to "pilfer my Likenefs, so I fhall pilfer his Scenes," anfwered he.

When, as a young Man, I had play'd *Hamlet*, in *Dublin*, this had never been the Life that I imagined for myfelf: to fhare in the creation of fuch horrible Filth. When I, at the abominable Text, began to gag and retch, for reading, in the Griffonage of *Sir Robert*, the moft Foul Thing that ever I heard of, I cried, "Egads, are you not "afhamed to commit fuch Things to Ink?"

"What does it matter?" anfwered *Sir Robert*. "It is not as if it's to be feen. One reading "to the Houfe is all it will have, and certainly not "with my Authorfhip acknowledged." — "Who, "then, fhall we proclaim is the Author of fuch "Filth?" — "You may fay it was given anonymoufly "by a Meffenger, for the Author wifhed to remain "unknown — and nobody could doubt that. Or elfe "we may blame it on that Rafcal, *Fielding,* for it's "fure that he could operate fuch Trouble. What's "fomething only *Fielding* would do?" — "Make "another tired Joke about *Farinelli,* the *caftrato*?" I fuggefted off-hand.

Sir Robert grinned at that, with his few remaining Teeth all bared, like chequered Tiles in a row. One perceived how the Maggot came crafhing through his Mind of a fudden. He began to write, giggling and tittering all the while; and before the Interval of five Minutes, he had completed a Scene. "How does that?" he afked, prefenting the finifh'd Page to me.

I took it, and, at what I read, I coloured like driven Snow. "'Sdeath, you will be hanged for "fimply reading that aloud," faid I.

And *Sir Robert's* only refponfe was to cackle like a *Bedlamite.*

We work'd at the Text for the next two Days, with fcarcely a Paufe for us to blink. *Sir Robert's* Servants brought Food and Refrefhment, which he at laft confented to let me eat of, tho' confequent of the vile and nafty Fantafications which he had infpired in my Brain thro' such villainous work, I fcarcely had a Stomach fit to be filled, left it fpew back outward.

When we had fcrowled out all of the difgufting *climax* of the Farce, I was fent to my Home for a good Night's Reft; and at laft I ate a quiet Supper with my own Wife and Children, all of whom had been placed under the Impreſſion that I was hired for a private Performance at the Eſtate of ſome great Nobleman, and hence my Days of Abſence. But tho' granted theſe few Hours of Repoſe, I was not yet free: for I was not only condemned to know *Sir Robert's* ſacrilegious reworking of the Coronation Hymn *Zadok the Prieſt* rattling inſide my Head the whole While, but moreover, I was due to ſee *Sir Robert* again on the Day to follow. On this next Occaſion, he put me to copy out his whole Manuſcript, so that it could be preſented by him, without Evidence that it was in his own Hand. After another day's drudgery on that Affair, I was ſummoned one more time to attend him; and it was on this Occaſion that I was told to join him at *Pall-Mall*. I could well ſuppoſe what was to be our Deſtination from that Place: and as I had ſuppoſed it ſhou'd be, *Sir Robert* pull'd me within *St. James's Palace* where we were to ſhew the "hideous diſcover'd Manuſcript."

Quite naturally the King, like all Men of Rank, when ever attending the Theatre, always took his ſeat upon the Stage itſelf, with all his Guardſmen and Courtiers, and the royal Box would diſrupt the Scenery and the Plan of Action, and it made one glad that his Majeſty was no Fanatick for the Theatre. But it was in this Context only, that I had ever known the Honour to obſerve his Majeſty. I had never been received at Court, nor done any Thing cloſe to the aforeſaid. Thus I was diſcovered ill at Eaſe, and I ſuppoſed that to enſure a becoming Entrance, I ſhould fancy myſelf to play a *role* as a Courtier, and make my beſt Affectations of what a Perſon in the Nobility might enact in this Circumſtance. *Sir Robert* watched me in theſe Endeavors, without Amuſement.

"What the Devil are you about, tripping to "and fro like a Ballet Dancer?" he aſked of me. "Only ſtand where you are, and be ſilent. I will aſk "of you a few Queſtions, and you ſhall anſwer them "ſimply, the way we have agreed — and that is "all."

Slumping, I went ſilent as a Stone, and thenceforth awaited only his Cues. We were in the King's perſonal Apartments. There was no Difficulty for us to enter, for the Prime Miniſter was a regular Viſitor, and known to all of the Guards and Secretaries without being given two Glances; and I was perceived as Part of his Gear on this Day. It was then but a Matter of awaiting the King to emerge, so that he might hear us.

I began to ſuppoſe that his Majeſty might preſent himſelf in the ſame Finery he wore when ever he was about the Town, or perhaps in even more royal Regalia than he would think to don when he was away from his Palace, ſuch as his Crown or his Ermine Robes. I was not only diſappointed, but flatly amazed, when out from a dark Chamber appeared a rather over-weight Man in a ſtate of Undreſs, wearing but a Turban and a Nightgown —

a fine one, but ſtill a mere Nightgown. This was the King. 'Tis no Marvel to me, now, that he ſhould have been Affronted by our Play, *Harlequin Shipwreck'd*, for our *King Oberon* had better Clothes than he.

When the Monarch ope'd his Mouth, he began to addreſs *Sir Robert* in *French*, but *Sir Robert* replied:

"If you pleaſe, Sire, for the ſake of Mr. "*Giffard* might we ſpeak in *Engliſh*?"

"**Very well**," replied the King, his *German* accent now moſt evident to me. It was heavy, deſpite his many Years in *England*. "**But what has dis Mr.** "**Giffard to do wid it?**" — "It was to Mr. *Giffard* "that the Text in queſtion was ſent," ſaid *Sir Robert* as he turned towards me. "Isn't that so?" he aſk'd.

For a Moment I found myſelf to ſtare ſtupidly, but then I manag'd a reply of a ſimple "Ay, "'tis so." This was what I had agreed to anſwer to any Thing *Sir Robert* would feign aſk.

"He brought it to me," continued *Sir Robert*, "and I have ſtraightaway brought it to you, "for it alarmed me every Bit as much as it did Mr. "*Giffard*."

"Ay, 'tis so," I replied automatically.

"**Is it worſe dan de Beggar's Opera?**" aſked the King. — "Much worſe," ſaid *Sir Robert*. — "**Worſe dan de Fall of Mortimer?**" — "Undoubtedly." — "**But it could not, certainly, be**

"**badder dan de Play=Shew where dey laught at me,**
"**de Harlequin Shipwreck'd?**"

At this I began to grow roſey with Shame, but the Miniſter continued in his Diſcourſe. He had born the freſh Manuſcript under his arm, and took it now to Hand. "Shall I read it to your Majeſty?"

"**Be so good,**" replied the King.

Already Shame-fac'd, I grew as red as a very Pulpit Cuſhion when *Sir Robert* read aloud the entire firſt Act of *The Golden Rump,* in all its abominable Satire. Even tho' I heard it now for the third Time, the Effect upon me was but little ſoftened. To the King, it was all new: his Face ſhewed ſtupified reactions to the Text's worſt Offenſes againſt Decency, but he ſaid Nothing, and he liſtened. Then came the ſecond Act, more pointed and more treaſonous than the firſt, and culminating at laſt on the dreadful *Farinelli* Scene. The King, at that, would hear no more; and this he marked by ſlamming his Fiſt upon a Table, then fiercely connecting his Gaze with that of the loweſt Perſon in the Room (this being myſelf) and then phyſically attacking this Man (myſelf) with ſavage Kicks and Blows. I ſcreamed for help, all confuſed and amazed; I could only think that his majeſty muſt have deciphered *Sir Robert's* Scheme, and of my Involvement as well, and that his Outrage was for that I had aſſiſted in the writing of so flagititous a Repreſentation.

Slick Filth.

I cried out Pleas for Forgiveneſs. Some Guards, hearing the Commotion, ſtepped into the Room; but the Miniſter ſignalled them not to worry themſelves. "It is only one of his Majeſty's uſual "reactions," ſaid *Sir Robert*. "He is only attacking a "Playwright. Have no Fear."

The Guards withdrew, and I was left to be pummeled, for I durſt not hit back at the King. I was aſtoniſh'd that this truly was how a Monarch conducted himſelf; and had ſome one put it up maliciouſly in a Satire, I ſhould have thought it were beyond Belief. Yet it was the Truth of this Man!

When at Laſt the royal Temper ſoftened, and he relented in his Attack, he left me upon the Floor at once very ſore and very ſtupid, but himſelf yet ſhrieking: "**I ſhall cut up every Theatre in "England by de Roots!**"

Tears in my eyes, I moaned, wiſhing to defend myſelf: "Your Majeſty, it was only *Sir* "*Robert's* idea ... " *Sir Robert* now took the turn to kick me. — "Be ſilent, you!"

He look'd again to the King. "Sire, I "apologiſe for him, he is unfamiliar with our Modes "of Conduct. He is an Actor, and you know they "are a crude Sort."

Never in a Century would I have ſtruck the King, but a mere Miniſter be he Prime or otherwiſe, was another Matter; and I nearly let him have one for that, but when I roſe, he ſtepped out of the way, and did not ſeem to even notice that I had meant to box his Ears. Meanwhile, the King perſiſted in his Fit. "**How can any man dare to write such Filth,** "**and conceive it fit to be played?**" cried he.

Sir Robert replied, "That is not for me, or "for Mr. *Giffard*, to ſay. The Text was ſent without "a Name — doubtleſs by a Man who wiſhed to "conceal his Identity for fear of your Majeſty's "Wrath." — "**Well he ought!**" ſaid the King. "**I** "**shall find the Scoundrel and hang him myself from** "**de Laundry-Pole!**"

"In order to prevent this Misfortune from "happening again," ſaid *Sir Robert*, "We ſhould "amend the Bill for the Licenſing of Theatres, to "include ſome Language that will addreſs the "Suppreſſion of any future offenſive Plays."

"**Can you not suppress dem now?**" aſked the King, his tone ſomething between Rage and Confuſion.

"I cannot, Sire. There is no Law that "requires Playwrights to gain Approval before "ſtaging what ever they like, and where ever they "like it. Nearly every Thing contained in *The* "*Golden Rump* would be Legal to put on the Stage, "to the preſent ſtanding of the Law."

At beſt his wording was deceptive — yes, one could perhaps Stage it, one time, before Word would get out and every one in the ſhew would be impriſon'd — but this was what the King needed to hear, in order to advance *Sir Robert's* Deſign.

"**Den yes!**" his Majeſty ſaid, "**Do what "ever you need, dat Noſſing so foul ſhall ever be "wrote again!**"

Sir Robert bowed. "Then I ſhall have it "arranged this Evening, your Majeſty."

The King expreſſed his Gratitude for the Miniſter's Vigilance and Aſſiſtance, after which he turned his Attention once again towards me. "**And "I apologiſe if I uſed you badly,**" he ſaid, "**but you "ſhould know dat ſuch a Work muſt fire my "Temper.**"

For my Part, I could compel no Reply but to nod very ſlowly, for I would not have a Pig like *Sir Robert* accuſe me of "crudeneſs" a ſecond Time.

At this *Sir Robert* bade his final *adieus* and then eſcorted me away, and not a Moment too ſoon. When we were again on to the Street, *Sir Robert* ſaid to me: "I have already prepar'd the "Paper-Work in expectation of his Majeſty's "Deciſion. It now ſhall only be a Matter of "preſenting everything to the Houſe. I pray they "ſhall react as badly as did his Majeſty." — "And "would you make of me a Rug for all the Houſe to "beat?" I ſnapp'd back at him with ſcorn. My Skin was colouring lavender in the Places where the King had ſtruck me.

"Your Part in this Operation is now "finiſhed," was the reply of *Sir Robert*. "Unleſs I "call for you again to confirm my Hiſtory — which "I doubt ſhall become neceſſary. So, go to your "Home, and ſay Nothing of what you've done. I "ſhall ſee you paid for the Work you have made, and "... well, if you can ever ſtage another Farce or "Droll or Tragedy again at *Goodman's-Fields*, after "the Paſſage of this Act, then perhaps I ſhall ſee "you at the Theatre."

With that, *Sir Robert* bade farewell to me, for the final Time. And for my Part, I ſwore to be aveng'd upon him.

That *Sir Robert* read the ſuppos'd Play to ſome Members of Parliament is ſure. I was not in attendance, and I know not Details of how it was enacted. I have heard ſaid of it, that there was much Affright and Horror amongſt the Lords, and that they ſpill'd a Deluge of Inquires ſuch as "How do "they chaſe the Queen's Clitoris-Ring about the "Stage?" and "How could the Actor burſt Semen all "over the Stage?" and "Would they truly dare to "incite a Rebellion againſt the Ariſtocracy on the "Stage?" and "Did they really find ſome one who "ſings like *Farinelli*?" Notwithſtanding a deliberate and blatant inſult to Lords *Pultney* and *Cheſterfield* which we inſerted into the Text, theſe ſame two

Men upheld themſelves as the moſt vocal Objectors to the propoſed Law, which was all as *Sir Robert* had expected. *Lord Cheſterfield* ſtood and gave an hour-long Speech, whereby he argued contrary to the Bill, tho' admitting that ſome inappropriate Plays had lately been performed:—

"I have, it is true, learned from common "Report without Doors, that a moſt ſeditious, a moſt "heinous Farce had been offered to one of the "Theatres, a Farce for which the Authors ought to "be puniſhed in the moſt exemplary Manner; but "what was the Conſequence? The Maſter of that "Theatre behaved as he was in Duty bound, and as "common Prudence directed: he not only refuſed to "bring it upon the Stage, but carried it to a certain "honourable Gentleman in the Adminiſtration, as "the ſureſt Method of having it abſolutely "ſuppreſſed. Could this be the Occaſion of "introducing ſuch an extraordinary Bill, at ſuch an "extraordinary Seaſon, and puſhing it in so "extraordinary a Manner? Surely no:— The dutiful "behaviour of the Players can never be a reaſon for "ſubjecting them to ſuch an arbitrary Reſtraint: it is "an Argument in their Favour, and a material one, "in my Opinion, againſt the Bill. Nay farther, if we "conſider all Circumſtances, it is to me a full Proof "that the Laws now in being are ſufficient for "puniſhing thoſe Players who ſhall venture to bring "any ſeditious Libel upon the Stage, and "confequently fufficient for deterring all Players "from acting any Thing that may have the leaft "tendency towards giving a reafonable Offence."

"But fuppofe, my Lords, it were neceffary "to make a new Law for the reftraining of the "Licentioufnefs of the Stage, which I am very far "from granting, yet I fhall never be for eftablifhing "fuch a Power as is propofed by this Bill. If Poets "and Players are to be reftrained, let them be "reftrained as other Subjects are, by the known "Laws of their Country; if they offend, let them be "tried as every *Englifhman* ought to be, by *God* and "their Country. Do not let us fubject them to the "arbitrary Will and Pleafure of any one Man. A "Power lodged in the Hands of one fingle Man, to "judge and determine, without any Limitation, "without any Control or Appeal, is a fort of Power "unknown to our Laws, inconfiftent with our "Conftitution. It is a higher, a more abfolute Power "than we truft even to the King himfelf; and "therefore I muft think, we ought not to veft any "fuch Power in his Majefty's *Lord Chamberlain.*"

"The laft Reafon I fhall trouble your "Lordfhips with for my being againft the Bill, is, "that in my Opinion, it will no way anfwer the End "propofed: To prevent the acting of a Play which "has any tendency to Blafphemy, Immorality, "Sedition, or private Scandal, can fignify Nothing, "unlefs you can likewife prevent its being printed "and publifhed. This Bill can therefore be of no ufe "for preventing either the Publick or the Private "injury intended by ſuch a Play; and conſequently "can be of no Manner of Uſe, unleſs it be deſigned "as a Precedent, as a leading Step towards another, "for ſubjecting the Preſs likewiſe to a Licenſer. For "ſuch a wicked Purpoſe it may, indeed, be of great "uſe; and in that Light, it may moſt properly be "called a Step towards arbitrary Power. Therefore I "muſt look upon the Bill now before us as a Step, "and a moſt neceſſary Step too, for introducing "arbitrary Power into this Kingdom: It is a Step so "neceſſary, that, if ever any future ambitious King, "or guilty Miniſter, ſhould form to himſelf so wicked "a Deſign, he will have Reaſon to thank us for "having done so much of the Work to his Hand; but "ſuch Thanks, or Thanks from ſuch a Man, I am "convinced every one of your Lordſhips would bluſh "to receive — and ſcorn to deſerve."

In Deſpite of the noble Speech, the Law was approved by the Houſe: all Theatres and Venues which offer Entertainment ſhould have to be Licenſed, and all new Texts for Plays be required ſhewn to the *Lord Chamberlain,* and approved by him, before they ſhould be ſtaged; and he may refuſe to grant his Approval for any Cauſe at all (ſuch as, if *Sir Robert* inſtructs him to withhold it.) I remember reading, with the utmoſt of Diſmay, that this was to go into effect on the 24th of *June.*

When I received the diſappointing News that the fatal Law had been paſſed becauſe of our (really, *Sir Robert's*) alleged Play, I knew I muſt make uſe of the deadly Inſtrument which had been left to me. *Sir Robert* had compoſed the moſt ſeditious, diſguſting, obſcene, ſhameful Thing I had ever ſeen in over forty Years of Life, a Work which ſatiriſed himſelf and all his Friends, as well as any Thing elſe which might be thought as ſacred. He had forced me to copy out the Text of his Play so that his Writing would not be recogniſed, nor his Part in its creation made apparent. In Conſequence, I ſtill poſſeſs'd the original Copy, writ in his Hand — tho' I told him I had burnt it. I could not riſque my own Theatre by a Performance of ſuch a Piece — for it was now required that I ſhould apply for a Licenſe to remain in Operation — nor could my moſt reſpectable Theatre ſuffice, for to perform this ſort of *Opus* ſhould require a Company that could not only learn their Lines in leſs than a Month, but who would not refuſe to perform ſuch vile Activities, as appearing naked and feigning themſelves *Anthropophagites*.

One of the Conſtituents of the new *Licenſing Act* was that it puniſhed as Vagrants thoſe itinerant Actors who performed about the Country at Fairs, (as well as now declaring that, by Law, Actors in all Unlicenſed Performances be alike to them in Rank.) It was thus amidſt this Outrage brewed, that I ſucceeded to locate a very agreeable *troupe* of *Harlequins* and *Columbines* who reſented the Miniſter's Actions, and deſpiſed the new Law, and who moreover did not perform under their own Names, and thereby were moſt content to take the Miniſter's Play where it could be beſt appreciated by the Publick.

Southwark Fair itſelf was often found to be in Conflict with the Law, for this Event was meant to run but for three Days in *September*, yet in Practice every Year it was begun in *June*, and it was ſtretched for many Weeks, to the Ire of all the Neighbourhood of *Southwark*. Yet this was to my Advantage, for I was determined to ſee *Sir Robert's* own Spectacle upon the Stage before the 24th of *June*. We rehearſed — Odsbodlikins, it took a real Genius to ſtage ſome of the Scenes (hey day, that damn'd Elephant!) but we were met with Succeſs, and for but one Night, *The Golden Rump* lived its monſtrous Life. Unluckily, we could not make a ſecond ſhew of it — the Authorities had been alerted after the premier. Yet, true to what *Sir Robert* had ſaid to the King, we were able to ſtage the Play the one Time; and Nothing could be proved about what we did in the firſt ſhew, only so long as there was not a ſecond ſhew. Methought that one ſhew was enough, in all Events: for a ſufficient number of People did obſerve *Sir Robert* to make ſport of himſelf, and his Brother too, as *Polecat*; enough ſaw the King made more than ſilly but flat-out ſickening; enough ſaw *Engliſh* politicks reduced to Group-Sodomy, by a Man who ſeems to know; and for myſelf, this help'd amend for a Few of the little Indignities to which the Miniſter, and his Minions, had ſubjected me.

And, as there is yet no Law againſt *printing* an Obſcene Play, as *Lord Cheſterfield* rightly obſerv'd it, I hope ye all ſhall enjoy the Opportunity to read preciſely what it was that *Sir Robert* wrote, in Order to grant himſelf the diabolical Power of banning all future Plays that could poſſibly give Offenſe to a Politician. Perhaps, juſt as the Laws of the *Romans, Celts, Feudal Knights* and *Papiſts* were all undone by the Hand of Time, so too, ſhall there ſome Day be an End made to the *Licenſing Act of 1737*.

THE GOLDEN RUMP.

DRAMATIS PERSONÆ.

GANYMEDE - A poor Link-Boy and He-Whore, lately made Secretary.

MAGICIAN *POLECAT* - King's Vizier and ſecret Enemy.

PRIESTESS *MESSALINA*.

KING *PILES* - a male *Soprano*.

FOYST - a Slave.

TURNKEY.

MESSENGER.

COURTIERS.

DANCERS.

TWO GUARDS.

PRISON GUARD.

PRISONERS.

GENTLEMAN.

PAUPER.

A BEAU.

LADIES OF THE BED-CHAMBER.

SLAVES.

ACT I.

Setting is a Temple within a Royal Palace, in the Figure of a great Buttocks, the Door which is the Entrance to the Stage being the *ſphinčter ani*. *Courtiers*, *Magician* and *Ganymede* enter together. *Ganymede* hath Pencil and a Note-Book.

MAGICIAN.

ome, come, Gentlemen! Whilſt the King is away in *Sauſageland* to attend his royal Duties there, I am in command of the Court and all of its Ceremony. The Time is come for the High Prieſteſs to adminiſter her ſacred Rites, that our Country of *Groſſ-Corruptia* may continue to thrive.

Enter the Prieſteſs, *holding a ſilver Bell and a Clyſter-Pipe of Gold. She rings the Bell, and all fall proſtrate before her and the Idol, but for the* Magician, *who hauls* Ganymede *back to his Feet.*

Riſe, riſe, for you are Part of our Sect and Ritual of the *Golden Rump Society.*

The Prieſteſs *rings the Bell again.*

PRIESTESS. Lo! Between thy golden Orbs reſts all that is good upon the Earth and in our Land. We pray to you and your holy Hole that we be kept in Security, Peace and good Health. Let no Evil fall upon our Land, nor upon our Seas, nor upon our Treaſury, nor our Bed-Sheets or Private Parts.

The Prieſteſs *begins to adminiſter liquid Gold into the Rump by means of the Pipe.*

With this Infuſion of *Aurum Potabile*, may your Might be ſtrengthened, your Bowels comforted, and your Complexion beautified like that of a hearty little Maiden.

MAGICIAN. You may now make your Petitions to the Pagod.

Courtiers *arrange themſelves before it.* Courtier 1 *kneels.*

COURTIER 1. O mighty and beautiful Fundament, pleaſe grant a Pardon for my Siſter who has given birth and then drowned the Infant, and now ſits in Gaol for the Crime.

The Golden Rump farts.

MAGICIAN. It is done. You may go.

Courtier 1 *ſteps away, and the ſecond takes his Place, kneeling.*

COURTIER 2. O glorious Windward Paſſage, I beg of you, relieve me of my Debts which have been incurred in the honeſt work of Gambling.

There is ſilence, and the Courtier *is diſmayed.*

No Reply? O I am undone!

MAGICIAN. Alas, the Rump cannot grant every Requeſt that is made of it. You may go.

The third Courtier *kneels.*

COURTIER 3. O your moſt glorious and ſplendiferous Roundneſs, I do humbly beſeech you to transform me into a Woman.

The Rump farts.

MAGICIAN. It is done. But now take this Woman away for ſhe appears improperly dreſſed before the Idol.

The two Courtiers *take away the third.*

PRIESTESS. Thus concludes the Viſion of the Rump!

The Prieſteſs *rings her Bell again and retreats.*

COURTIER 4. Mr. *Ganymede*, you do not mark your Paper, tho' it is your Duty to record the Miracles granted by the Rump. Surely you muſt take Note of what hath tranſpired?

GANYMEDE. Be there any Thing of Note or no, I am not equipped to render it.

COURTIER 4. How so?

GANYMEDE. Why, I cannot read nor write.

COURTIER 4. Cannot read nor write! But you are Secretary, how have you come upon this Place if you cannot mark our Words?

GANYMEDE. The Magician hath chofen me on his own Account, and when I did make the fame Objection that you now do, he replied that I oughtn't concern myfelf, and that I fhould moft naturally acquire the Learning neceffary, with Time and Practice.

COURTIER 4. Your Awfulnefs, how can this be so?

MAGICIAN. If you think my Choice amifs, then to the Chopping-Block with you for Treafon.

COURTIER 4. Alas! Nay, I voice no Difagreement, I merely afk your Method be difclofed.

MAGICIAN. That is not for you to know, unlefs you purchafe a Place within my Cabinet. Tickets are for fale within the Coffee-Houfe acrofs the Way, called *The Prick*, which you fhall know by the Image above its Door.

COURTIER 4. Of a Needle?

MAGICIAN. Of a great Dildo.

COURTIER 4. Alas, I am tapp'd dry after this Election laſt when I bought my Seat at Court, but I ſhall ſee what I can raiſe by pimping one of my Daughters.

Exit Courtier.

GANYMEDE. Your Awfulneſs, I muſt profeſs that I too am puzzled by your Choice of me for this courtly Poſition. I am but a poor Link-Boy, but now with all the Streets alight my Trade is near extinction; and I, grown too large to carry Men's Tapers in my Hands, took to bear them in ſome other Parts.

MAGICIAN. Now, that we are alone, Mr. *Ganymede*, I may explain to you my Purpoſe for employing you thus at Court. As you know, you have every Reaſon to truſt yourſelf with me. Thus I confide to you in Confidence that you poſſeſs a peculiar Trait which advances you so much in my Eſteem that I nearly dare to ſay you are invaluable to me. You now have born witneſs to the Ceremony of extorting Favours from the Golden Rump, but what if I told that there is a Manner even more ſure to provoke his Boons and Graces?

GANYMEDE. I think it would be to the Country's greateſt Advantage.

MAGICIAN. To Hell with the Country! *Groſſ-Corruptia* may rot and wither to an Otomy so long as I can pound ſome *Mummia Falſa* from it to ſell to the *Turks* or the *French* or the *London Exchange* as I have done so many Times before.

GANYMEDE. Ay, by your Treachery, so many Lords are left pennileſs that they can no more afford my modeſt Prices, and thus every Duke, Earl, and Viſcount were left merely to rape me in the Back Alleys.

MAGICIAN. Indeed, but now I have lifted you from that Life that you may have your Revenge on 'em. Look here. Look upon this Idol of the Golden Rump.

The Magician *begins to fondle it.*

Touch it now, you may touch it.

Ganymede touches it and a giant mechanical Phallus ſprings upward.

GANYMEDE. Zounds! Have I broken it?

MAGICIAN. Nay, nay, my Lad. You ſee, the true Power of the Idol lies not in the Rump alone but in the Yard. And 'tis you alone that hath power to awaken this Golden Yard. This I knew the Moment I laid my Sight upon you, for it is ſaid in Prophecy: *Cacadoodoo cunny bumfuck*, which, tranſlated from the Antient Tongue means, *The Boy with the fineſt Arſe ſhall provoke the Ardor*, and you, good Sir, have as fine a one as ever I did ſee. Pray, drop your Breeches and let me look upon it.

Ganymede *drops Breeches.*

Put it to Teſt. Whilſt holding it, make a Petition that we ſhould have a marvelous Dance performed before us, by the fineſt Dancers in all the Land.

GANYMEDE. O mighty Tarſe, give unto me my fond Deſire, that we ſee Dancers finer than ever ſeen in *Sadler's Wells*.

MAGICIAN. Simpleton!

A Company of Dancers *appear on ſtage and dance. Exit* Dancers.

Behold the Power of the Rod! The Prophecy ſaith, *Cockencod bubbies prickiwicki piſſen bed*, which is to ſay, that once that Golden Rod be in my Power, Nothing can demean myſelf nor the High Prieſteſs. Now that this Aim is achieved, you ſhall be rewarded fully — I'll ſee to it your Execution is diſpatch'd with Speed! Guards, Guards!

GANYMEDE. What treachery is this?

Two Guards *enter.*

MAGICIAN. Take this Raſcal away for Execution. You ſee he hath dropped his Breeches before the Pagod.

GUARD 1. Such Sacrilege! Indeed, the Wretch ſhall not go unpuniſhed.

The Guards *ſeize* Ganymede *and take him away, his Breeches ſtill down.*

GANYMEDE. Alas! This is my Reward for having faith in Miniſters of the Crown!

Ganymede *is taken away. Alone, the* Magician *tries to pull the Phallus but ſoon as he touches it, it retracts.*

MAGICIAN. Blaſt and bugger! It ſeems I ſhall have further need of that Bardiſh, for even once provok'd, his Touch alone ſhall keep the Rod erect. But alas, now that I have been thus expoſed, how am I to regain his Love and Confidence?

Exit Magician. *Enter* Prieſteſs.

PRIESTESS. Alas! The Prieſteſſes of our Nation bear so many greater Woes than others. While wiſely ſome Lands prohibit their Prieſteſſes from amatory and carnal Purſuits, it is our Liberty in *Groſſ-Corruptia* to indulge in aptly named Libertinage. But the Gentleman who has taken my Fancy loves another — and is faithful! Curſe it. I ſhould wiſh for the Great Golden Rump to ſtrike my Rival dead, or puniſh her with a Pox for so wicked a Theft as to claim what was rightly mine. It is in my Power to ſee it done, for in my poſſeſſion is a magical Ring which, when wiſely uſed, will enſure the Favours of the Idol be always granted, when ever aſk'd, with no Debate nor Delay. But no. I am too ſoft of Heart to aſk so vile a Deed, tho' Temptation burns at my Breaſt. I muſt diſtract myſelf. I ſhall immerſe myſelf in ſome charitable Aċt, and perhaps the ſweetneſs of the Deed will ſweeten, too, my Temper. To the Priſon I ſhall go, to beſtow ſome Bleſſings upon the poor Souls in that Place. For it is a comfort in Times of Woe to ſee others who ſuffer, and 'tis ſure, Gaols are ever my Obſeſſion. Perhaps ſome White Knight who ſaves the poor diſtreſſed Damſels from ſwinging, by pleading their Bellies, can render Service to me in ſome Interval.

Exit Prieſteſs.

ACT II.

In the Prifon, with a felection of Chains upon the Wall. *Prifon Guard* and a *Gentleman*, and a *Turnkey*. Barred Chambers are about with *Prifoners* within, and *Ganymede* in one.

PRISON GUARD.

Here we are, Sir. Now choofe yourfelf a pair of Fetters from the Wall.

GENTLEMAN. I cannot fay I like the Looks of any of them.

PRISON GUARD. Certainly, Sir. Why, with thofe Lace Sleeves I fhould think they'd make a fhabby Pairing. Everything is within the Reach of a Gentleman fuch as yourfelf, methinks. A fine delicate pair fuch as thefe, for inftance, coft a full Guinea.

GENTLEMAN. So I fee. And what Price for a fet of fuch Delicacy that they cannot be feen at all, if you underftand me?

PRISON GUARD. Two Guineas would do, for fuch a fine Man as yourfelf.

The Gentleman *pays the money, and the* Guard *uſhers him over to the* Turnkey.

Thanks, good Sir. And if there is any more I can do to ſerve your Grace, do not heſitate to requeſt me.

The Turnkey *and* Gentleman *exit. Enter a* Pauper *in rags.*

Fie! I can ſee by the Looks of you, you are Waſted Space. Why I ſhould be in Luck to gain a Farthing from a viſiting Wife for you.

Guard *puts heavy chains upon him and ſhoves him away to the* Turnkey. *Enter a* Beau.

A Newcomer? Nay, I know you well enough. Welcome Home, good Sir.

BEAU. So good to ſee you again, Sir. Your Servant, ever.

PRISON GUARD. Your Servant.

BEAU. I think I ſhould like a Room with a pleaſing View from the Window, and the Floor well waſhed with Perfume before I enter.

PRISON GUARD. Excellent, Sir. Come right this Way and I ſhall place you thither myſelf.

Exit the Priſon Guard *and* Beau. *Enter the* Prieſteſs.

PRIESTESS. What, no Guard to greet me? Fie, I fancy that the Raſcal of a Guard hath been paid to eaſe on another Eſcape, by his abſence. Be it so, I ſhall be at Leiſure to viſit whom I may.

She ſtops before Priſoner 1.

Well met, Sir. What cauſe hath brought you here to-day?

PRISONER 1. Alas! I am undone! I have been placed hither by ſome Lout, for I dared to ſeek his Aſſaſſination.

PRIESTESS. Was it in a Duel?

PRISONER 1. Nay, for I am no like Rank to ſuch a Man. I fired my Piſtol at the King himſelf, before his departure to *Sauſageland*. But damn me, I did miſs his Heart by a Yard, and only kill'd a Maſter of the Bed-Chamber.

PRIESTESS. Ay, for thoſe are cheaply had as Street-Sweeps. But O! You are so fair of Face and so handſome in your Youth! I cannot dare to think about so fine a Figure, ſhamefully hanged and carved up as an Otomy! Nay, you muſt uſe your Face and Figure, and what ever elſe you have with you, while you may. I ſhall enſure your Pardon.

PRISONER 1. Madam, is it in your Power?

PRIESTESS. Certes, for I poſſeſs an Influence with the Golden Rump.

PRISONER 1. Praiſe be upon you! What ever can repay this Debt?

PRIESTESS. O, I ſeek only ſimple Pleaſures. Come you up to my Cloiſter, and ſee me. Every Night, I am at ready. O Turnkey! Come come!

The Turnkey *comes.*

Releaſe this beautiful Youth at once. His Age ſhould ſpare him for his Crime. Come, as I command! You know my Influence with the Golden Rump is paſt all Meaſure.

The Turnkey *opens the Cell and releaſes the* Priſoner, *who runs off.* Prieſteſs *gives a Coin to the* Turnkey.

And who is next to pique my Intereſt? Ho there, Sir. Tell me of your Crime.

PRISONER 2. Alas! Fair Lady, I am impriſoned for a Crime againſt Nature.

PRIESTESS. Of what ſort?

PRISONER 2. I ſhall recount my ſorry Tale! You ſee, by profeſſion I am a Poet, and as I came from my favourite Coffee-Houſe, I chanced to ſpy a moſt comely Creature, a fair Maid ſitting upon an Aſs in the Lane. She was a ſeller of Merkins and Dildos, and ſhe cried out for ſome one to let her demonſtrate her worldly Wares. I ſpoke to her, fair Thing ſhe was, and wiſh'd that ſhe would be my *Muſe* for my next Sonnet. But ſhe ſat unmoved, or at leaſt unconvinced, with my Worthineſs, and so ſhe requeſted I firſt demonſtrate my Skills to her. I thus read to her my neweſt Poem, which did go:

As ſlain by Sun, so falls the Night,
Quell'd within ſome ſtarry Blight:
We too, are ſtruck within the Fight,

As Dark o'ertakes the Sun so bright.
Salvation, for the which you pine;
Flares once then dies; and so does mine,
'Tis ſmother'd out by Velvet fine,
Finer ſtill than Velvetine.
SOTERIA *cannot endure,*
When THANATOS *is only Cure.*
How couldſt thou break a Love so pure:
Your Soul and Heart are black, obſcure.
O SISYPHUS, *our way is loſt!*
Thus 'twixt, 'twixt Shadows be we toſſ'd.
THANATOS, THANATOS.

PRIESTESS. And it was not for your Poetry you were put in Gaol?

PRISONER 2. No, never. Some one in the Royal Houſe loves Poetry too well.

PRIESTESS. Then I muſt let you out, for if that was not a Crime then neither can be ſaid of what ever elſe you've done. I need hear no more of your Tale. Turnkey! Come hither.

Turnkey *comes and lets out* Priſoner 2.

PRISONER 2. Thanks, Madam, a thouſand Times. I ſhall ſee you made immortal in a Sonnet for this!

PRIESTESS. Be only certain that it is of a bawdy ſort.

PRISONER 2. I ſhall.

He goes. Prieſteſs *gives* Turnkey *another Coin. She goes to* Ganymede's *Door.*

PRIESTESS. Bleſs me! What is this fine Thing before me? I ſhould think a Creature of ſuch Beauty ought have more Viſitors than that criminal *Robert Walpole* the *Engliſh* Miniſter ever had, when he was in the *Tower.* Turnkey, open this Door!

The Turnkey *comes.*

TURNKEY. Madam, I ſhould wiſh Nothing better than to open this door, but I am under the expreſs Direction of *Polecat* the Magician not to let this Raſcal out, no matter how great the Bribe.

PRIESTESS. No matter the Bribe? Why what has been his Crime?

TURNKEY. He hath inſulted the Pagod of the Golden Rump.

PRIESTESS. Alas! Then ope the Door, but only that I may join inſide with him.

Turnkey *diſcloſes the door and* Ganymede *is diſcovered with his Arſe to the Audience.*

That will do. Now leave us.

Prieſteſs *gives him a Coin. She and* Ganymede *meet in the door. She ſlaps him on the Rump.*

God damn that is one fine Arſe! I ſhould like Nothing better than to lick it.

GANYMEDE. And so you ſhall, my Dear.

Ganymede *puts his hand up her Skirt.*

PRIESTESS. Take Caution, or you ſhall find the magick Ring with which I keep control of the Golden Rump.

GANYMEDE. O a Plague upon that Golden Rump! It is only for its Sake I am here, and not even a Duke or a Smuggler hath ready Caſh enough to pay the ceaſeleſs Duties and Fees of the Guards. Why none could pay ſuch Fines but a Guard himſelf!

PRIESTESS. Then perhaps I can be of Aſſiſtance to you. True, my own Bed is much more fine and warm than the ſorry Straw you lay upon in here. Let us go, and I will uſe my Power to ſecure your Releaſe, notwithſtanding the wiſhes of that ſilly old Magician, who calls me a fat Bitch when he thinks I do not hear him.

GANYMEDE. But what if they aſk you whither we go?

PRIESTESS. I ſhall ſay that it is to try an inoculation on you.

GANYMEDE. Pox?

PRIESTESS. Do not you malign me!

Exit Prieſteſs *and* Ganymede. *Enter the* Magician *and the* Priſon Guard.

MAGICIAN. So you muſt underſtand that, notwithſtanding my prior Command, the Circumſtance hath been altered. *Ganymede* muſt go free.

PRISON GUARD. But what could ſee a Pardon for ſuch a Crime as that which was done by him?

MAGICIAN. I oppofed his doing it, but the Publick demand for his Expofure of his two *South-Sea Bubbles* was more than could be politely refufed by him or any good Man, so tho' it was before the Idol and againft our Law, not he but thofe who put him up to it fhould be blamed.

He gives money to the Guard.

PRISON GUARD. Well, I cannot oppofe any Thing which so greatly enhances my own Wealth. I fuppofe then it is as you fay — but look'ee! What is this? He is gone!

MAGICIAN. Duplicitous Rafcal, you have not taken a Bribe to let him loofe, have you?

PRISON GUARD. I fwear on't I have done no fuch Thing, in this particular Cafe. What ever means he hath ufed are as great an affront to me as to you, for I am robbed of my rightful Bribe! I muft get to the bottom of this! I'll fmoke the one behind it all!

Exit Prifon Guard.

MAGICIAN. Alas! and Alack! Alackaday! Mother-Fucker! I well may be ruined in my Scheme, for lacking *Ganymede's* Power I cannot control the Golden Rump and Yard as I would. Only one other knows as much Power over the Rump as myſelf — and this is the fat Bitch Prieſteſs *Meſſalina*. She alone is my Rival! I can only pray that ſhe does not come into it, or all ſhall be as I feared. Every body knows that Women are all Strumpets and Whores, and even one's own Mother is no better than a Suck-Prick in a Gutter, and Wives as well. I hope that there be no Women in my preſence to bleed all over the Seats with their Menſtruations!

Exit Magician.

INTERLUDE:

A Scene of the King *in* Sauſageland, *with his* Miſtreſſes *and* Boys. *He is so great and fat he cannot walk and muſt be wheeled in by an Elephant that ſcarce can pull him. A* Boy *bangs his Prick on a Timpani. The* King *ſings like* FARINELLI, *to the Tune of* SON QUAL NAVE CH'AGITATA.

KING.

I ſhould like to fuck like VULCAN;
Tho' it make my Wife a bold Whore,
She can ſwive one, well as good and all can.
She will nevermore
Be begrudg'd to Love of mine.
I would not have my Taſtes perplex;
I will bugger one or both Sex,
For I find them both so fine.

The Boys *ſurround the* King *like a Fountain and piſſ on him, to his Delight. Exeunt omnes.*

ACT III.

A Garden with many Shrubs and Paths. Sparſely dreſſed *Men* and *Women* emerge or chaſe each other into and out of the Buſhes. The *Magician* emerges from a Buſh, wiping his Mouth with his Hand.

MAGICIAN.

Well, I have bagpip'd every man with a Seat in Parliament so 'tis ſure my Bills ſhall paſs now.

Enter Courtier 2.

COURTIER 2. Well met, Your Awfulneſs. I am your Servant.

MAGICIAN. Do you come to ſpeak or to ſwive?

COURTIER 2. Why not both? You know that I am in dire Straits. I want Money badly. So I have been ſelling my ſelf as a Bardiſh.

MAGICIAN. Is there good Money in it?

COURTIER 2. I have thus far earned ten Guineas and a Farthing.

MAGICIAN. What, a Farthing! What niggardly Skin-Flint gave you that?

COURTIER 2. All did, Sir!

MAGICIAN. Zounds! At that Price I can not refiſt the Bargain. Come back here and I ſhall try you.

They go into a Buſh, Magician *is left peering over the Top while the* Courtier *is bent below him. Enter* Ganymede *and the* Prieſteſs.

GANYMEDE. What need have we for Gardens? Your Bed is fit enough, and certain that no Graſs grows upon it.

PRIESTESS. It is well when I am virtuous, but when I act the Strumpet I am *virtuoſo*, and any ſuch Performer needs an Audience, that the Talent be not waſted.

GANYMEDE. It is a Waſte only if you perform but for yourſelf. With me, you have a ready Accompaniment.

PRIESTESS. Singer and Fiddler. Now ſhew me that Bow of yours. Indeed, you have no Reaſon to be aſhamed before an Audience. That lengthy Beam ſhall ſuffice to ſcrape my Catgut. Yes, yes, ſtrike my E-String! Fill me with Roſin!

They ſtart to copulate, and the Magician *ſees.*

MAGICIAN. What do I ſee, *Ganymede* and the *Prieſteſs*? Alas! She alone can match my Power in this Kingdom — would I knew the Reaſon why.

PRIESTESS. Caution, *Ganymede*, or you ſhall diſlodge my magick Ring with which I can command the Golden Rump and Yard.

MAGICIAN. So that is it! Now I know how this Woman hath had Power to outwit me all theſe Years.

COURTIER 2. By God's Wounds, muſt you ſoliloquize even as you fuck me? Talk at leaſt of ſome Erotick Thing.

MAGICIAN. I am harder for that magick Ring of hers than for your overſtretched Arſe. An Elephant would prove more taut.

COURTIER 2. Blame me not when the Trouble is you lack the Stuff to fill the Space.

Ganymede *frigs* Prieſteſs *as he fucks her.*

PRIESTESS. O yes, *Ganymede*! Frig me as thoſe *Engliſhmen*, *Cheſterfield* and *Pultney*, do to one another when they are alone!

GANYMEDE. Ay! You can ſay it becauſe it is but your Opinion within our Shew — here in the Garden. Any Lawyer will declare as much.

PRIESTESS. Speak filthy, vile Things to me!

GANYMEDE. *Ich Dien. Ich Dien.*

PRIESTESS. O, I die too! Ah!

MAGICIAN. There! I glimpſe it between her Legs, the Ring of which ſhe ſpeaks. It is like an Ear-Bauble, but run through her Clitoris.

GANYMEDE. What, you would leave me ſtill unfiniſh'd?

PRIESTESS. Nay. My Ladies of the Bed-Chamber are here for that.

Enter Ladies of the Bed-Chamber, *and they all at once fondle, ſuckle and frig* Ganymede.

Alas, poor *Ganymede*, I am a buſy Woman with many Duties to attend, so I muſt leave you with theſe capable Nymphs. Do come to ſee me again later, if you have the Opportunity.

GANYMEDE. Let theſe fair Creatures do their worſt, I ſhall be ready again for you by to-night.

Exit Prieſteſs. Magician *ſends* Courtier *away.*

MAGICIAN. Away with you, I've had my Farthing's worth.

Exit Courtier.

Perhaps I can ſpeak with *Ganymede* whilſt he lays diſtracted. Through him, the Key to all the Country reſts. Good Afternoon, good Sir. Your Servant.

GANYMEDE. *Polecat*! Why ſhould you be here?

MAGICIAN. I come to make my Apology, for there was ſome Miſunderſtanding between us before. I haſtened to the Priſon to ſee you freed, truly I did, but when I arrived I diſcovered that you had already been let out.

GANYMEDE. I am much diſtracted now, I cannot ſpeak.

MAGICIAN. O, let me help you there.

Magician *frigs* Ganymede, *who is delighted.*

GANYMEDE. O! O! Ladies, leave off, he really is much better at it. The Man knows what he does.

MAGICIAN. Yes, I do it often enough that I ought to know.

The Ladies *leave.* Magician *remains frigging* Ganymede, *and they talk though* Ganymede *is diſtracted.*

I muſt make my Apology to you for my paſt Affront. It was all a great Miſtake, and I hope to make Reparation.

GANYMEDE. Be it so? I cannot complain.

MAGICIAN. But I cannot think what Help I can grant, when it ſeems you have befriended the High Prieſteſs ſince laſt I ſpoke with you ...

GANYMEDE. Keep your Hand at work, I am almoſt there.

MAGICIAN. My Hand is ready to ſerve as you require. But know you, it ſhould have been unneceſſary would the Prieſteſs have finiſh'd you off.

GANYMEDE. She is very buſy.

MAGICIAN. Indeed ſhe is! But like all Women, ſhe can be induced to make more Time for you, if only you engage her in the proper way.

GANYMEDE. How's that?

MAGICIAN. Why, with Preſents! Bribes, as we ſay in Politics. Men and Women both are bought so readily, you know. Find a Gift ſhe would delight in ... take, for inſtance, her favourite Ring. You know the one, that ſhe keeps on her? Have it ſet with fine Gems, to render it ſtill more brilliant on her Body.

GANYMEDE. That might be beyond my Means.

MAGICIAN. Give the Ring to me and I ſhall overſee the work. It is as much as I can do to amend the Trouble I made for you before.

GANYMEDE. But why ſhould you ſeek to do me ſuch a favour — O! Proceed, proceed.

MAGICIAN. Why? You remember what I ſhewed you. You alone can control the Idol. I confeſs, indeed, I have my own Motives in this (ſince my Friendſhip with you can advance us both) but alſo I ſhould not wiſh that you think ill of me, for it was so ſhameful an Errour that I made before.

GANYMEDE. How can I be aſſured you'll not make a like Errour?

MAGICIAN. I ſhall make you, here and now, a genuine Lord. With this Title you can be aſſured protection, for you know I am not a Nobleman myſelf, and thus I cannot have

Power over you once you are fixed at higher Rank.

GANYMEDE (*impaſſioned.*) Very good, very good. O!

Ganymede *comes off. There is an immenſe quantity of Semen. Every one is coated and ſtained by it.*

MAGICIAN. Now that you are at eaſe, let us get on with the Ceremony.

Magician *licks Semen from his Fingers, then whiſtles a ſignal. Enter* Slaves, *one holding a Chamber-Pot, another with a Paddle.*

You will be a Marqueſs, but you muſt paſs *Groſſ-Corruptia's* antient Rite of Paſſage. You muſt be fully ſmacked with a Paddle, a Score, and then you ſhall drink the Contents of this *Pot de Chambre.*

GANYMEDE. To drink it?

MAGICIAN. I aſſure you, Sir, you ſhall know more Shit in your Mouth once you argue in the Houſe of Lords.

Ganymede *begins the ritual. One* Slave *ſpanks him as he drinks the Chamber-Pot, he being revolted and groaning as he does, but he ſucceeds and completes the Ritual. The* Magician *preſents him a Badge.*

I now declare you — in abſence of the King — Marqueſs of *Bumfuck.*

The Slaves *applaud.* Ganymede *ſtrives not to vomit.*

GANYMEDE. O my Belly ſwells!

MAGICIAN. Folly! Men cannot bear Children no matter how much they are buggered.

GANYMEDE. I mean I am ill, you Ninny.

MAGICIAN. The Feeling will paſs. Meantime, I ſhall ſend a Slave to collect the Ring from the Prieſteſs. *Foyſt*! Go to the Prieſteſs and bring us back the Ring ſhe keeps dangling from her Cunt. Tell her, if needed, that it is *Ganymede* who wiſhes to have it.

Exit Slave.

Since you are a new made Lord, perhaps you ſhould exerciſe your Skill. Let us debate, for the ſake of Practice. Tell me your Argument in favour of eating the Babies of the Poor.

Ganymede *vomits.*

A perfect argument. You will be a Member of the Cabinet one day. But of courſe you will, for that Power over the Golden Rump which your own glorious Rump proffers, will enſure as much for you.

GANYMEDE. Is it of ſuch Value? I did formerly rent it out for a few Shillings a go.

MAGICIAN. There are Lords who let theirs for a Farthing, I aſſure you; and Ladies who take Nothing at all, which, if you aſk me, renders 'em worſe than Whores, for their lack of Wit. Why, it is but Animals that ſwive without receiving ſome greater Trade!

GANYMEDE. But I think the Prieſteſs, *Meſſalina,* loves me; even tho' her Love be too great in volume to pour entirely upon one Diſh.

MAGICIAN. Perhaps, with your Power, we may approach the Golden Rump and ſee that Marriage ſhall be permitted between multiple People at once, as the *Turks* and Slaves are ſometimes wont to do.

GANYMEDE. A fine Conceit!

MAGICIAN. And we ſhall ſee forward a Law that Men can marry Dogs, and Snakes, and what ever Creature captures their Fancy. For really, is a Woman any better than either?

GANYMEDE. But then can Women too wed Animals?

MAGICIAN. I ſuppoſe if they propoſe the Marriage.

Enter Foyſt *the ſlave, breathleſſ and holding a Ring.*

FOYST. Sir, as done, I have acquired the Ring from Prieſteſs *Meſſalina*. When firſt I aſked, ſhe was unwilling to yield it to me, but ſhe put ſome other Materials on offer, and in the courſe of their examination I was able to pilfer it from her.

MAGICIAN. That is excellent, Foyſt. I ſhall refrain from beating you for many Days for this. And now I have the control of both

Means to move the Pagod. But before I make too great an haſte in revealing myſelf to *Ganymede* again, I ſhall enſure both he and the Prieſteſs are nullified of any Threat to me. I ſhall ſee them both dead before the Night is through.

He goes to Ganymede.

Come come, my Friend. Let us haſten to the Palace, where celebration is in order. You are, after all, now a Nobleman.

Exeunt.

ACT IV.

Scene 1. A Room in the Palace decorated with erotick Paintings. The *Courtiers* form a queue in which each buggers the Man before him and is buggered by one behind. Nude *Dancers* trip about as they ſing, ZADOK THE PRIEST.

COURTIERS.

To Heaven we'll go, and bugger the
Angels, indulging Sodomy's Whim.
We'll frig their Tarſes, and ſwive and fuck Arſes;
We'll frig, and ſwive, and fuck, and then:
Cods ſhall run dry, then out we cry,
"We are fucked divinely, amen, alleluia."

Enter Magician *with* Ganymede *on a Leaſh.*

MAGICIAN. O I ſee Parliament is in Seſſion! Go join, *Ganymede.*

Ganymede *walks toward, but is hindered by the Leaſh.*

GANYMEDE. Why muſt I have this on?

MAGICIAN. You muſt have it till you are trained well enough to follow my Commands without. It is as the others do.

COURTIER 1 (*announcing.*) In abſence of the King, his Awfulneſs the great Magician *Polecat* ſhall ſtand in for his Majeſty.

COURTIER 2 (*to* Magician.) We have been in debate of a Bill to hang every body in *Scotland.*

MAGICIAN. Pooh! Why hang them all when 'tis more thrifty to ſtarve them? I do not ſupport this. *Ganymede*, make the Argument.

GANYMEDE. What he ſaid.

MAGICIAN. Very good! In view of this great Objection, the Bill is now poſtponed indefinitely, till it can be reviſited. (*He calls out.*) *Foyſt! Foyſt!* I am weak with hunger. Bring me ſome Suſtenance. Yes! The Heads of unwanted Babies.

Enter Foyſt *with a Baſket of ſevered Babies' Heads.* Magician *begins to eat them like they are Apples.*

COURTIER 2. The next Bill for debate is to procure Money for the reſculpting of all Statues which depict clothed Men, to inftead be nude.

MAGICIAN. Quite neceffary, efpecially in the Churches. I give my Affent to this. It is paffed.

COURTIER 2. The next Bill to command that all Priefts in Churches, who are clothed Men, be nude.

MAGICIAN. This fhall require Confideration, for not all Priefts are well-formed enough for me to frig myfelf at the Sight of.

COURTIER 3. Ay, and until we are able to infert more handfome Priefts I think this Bill is beft poftponed.

MAGICIAN. On this we are agreed.

COURTIER 2. And the final Bill for the Day, is one which feeks to eftablifh a new Tax upon the Poor, to provide for thofe of them which are in need with Nourifhment, which fhall confift of Poifon of adequate Strength to kill a ftrong Bull.

MAGICIAN. I think it is a very efficient Strategy. Are there any Objections?

No? Then I grant my Aſſent. It is paſſed. Let us end the Buſineſs for this Day.

Exeunt Courtiers *and* Slaves.

GANYMEDE. I will profeſs to have fancied that the Life of a Lord would be ſomething more enviable than this.

MAGICIAN. Do you ſay you find Lordſhip unſatisfying?

GANYMEDE. It is but Servitude in another Guiſe.

MAGICIAN. Indeed. The Depths of which you ſhall come to know but now.

Enter Prieſteſs, *held by* Foyſt. *She is tied up as if a Priſoner.*

PRIESTESS. Help! Help! I have been abducted!

GANYMEDE. Prieſteſs! What is the meaning behind this, *Polecat*?

MAGICIAN. You can command the Golden Rump, and ſhe has had the Influence of the Magick Ring, but which I have ſtolen away.

He difplays the Ring.

With you and the Prieftefs caft afide, I alone will command the Golden Rump.

PRIESTESS. Do you mean to murder us?

MAGICIAN. Yes, but I fhall make it feem as if your Death was at *Ganymede's* Hand, and he a jealous Lover.

GANYMEDE. And what of my Fate?

MAGICIAN. I fhall fay I killed you in defenfe of the Prieftefs, but I was too late to fave her. Then, I fhall have you ftuffed and mounted like a Stag, your Arfe forever preferved so it can continue its hold over the Golden Rump. It will hang upon my Wall in the Drawing Room, above the Side-Board where we keep the *Pot de Chambre.*

GANYMEDE. Unfpeakable Rogue!

Ganymede *leaps at the* Magician *and knocks the Ring from his Hand. It rolls away.*

MAGICIAN. O, you Fool! Now the Ring is loſt. Who knows whom ſhall recover it?

GANYMEDE. Slave, purſue that Ring and you ſhall have your Freedom!

Foyſt *releaſes the* Prieſteſs *and chaſes the Ring.*

PRIESTESS. Nay, I ſhall have it firſt!

Prieſteſs *follows in chaſe.* Exeunt.

MAGICIAN. Fie! Well, I ſtill have you upon a Leaſh. To the Pagod, and I ſhall requeſt of him my favours with your Power.

Exeunt omnes.

Scene 2. The Buttocks-ſhaped Temple. The Golden Rump at center.

Enter Magician *and* Ganymede, *hauled on his Leaſh.*

MAGICIAN. Dawdle not. This Way, hence.

Magician *poſitions* Ganymede *before the Idol and tears away his Breeches. The Idol reacts with the extenſion of the Wand.*

GANYMEDE. I ſhall never help you! Never!

MAGICIAN. O great and powerful Idol of the Golden Rump, grant me your Bleſſings. It is my Wiſh —

Ganymede *tries to get away, entangles the* Magician *in the Leaſh. Enter* Prieſteſs *and* Foyſt *together. The* Prieſteſs *holds the Ring.*

PRIESTESS. Fear not, *Ganymede*! I have recovered the Ring!

MAGICIAN (*to the Idol.*) — My Wiſh be that the Prieſteſs ſhall die!

The Rump farts accord.

GANYMEDE. Haſten, Prieſteſs! Uſe your Ring to wiſh for Leniency!

MAGICIAN. She ſhall not!

Magician *leaps towards her but is withheld by* Ganymede's *weight on the Leaſh. He is forced to releaſe* Ganymede's *Leaſh to run to the* Prieſteſs, *from whom he ſnatches the Ring.*

PRIESTESS. O I feel faint ...

MAGICIAN. The Ring is now mine!

GANYMEDE. Ay, but you have loſt my fine Arſe!

Ganymede *rubs it on the Idol.*

O great Golden Rump, do not Rump me in my Requeſt. Have Mercy upon the Prieſteſs and let her live.

The Rump farts. The Prieſteſs *begins to recover.*

PRIESTESS. My Blood flows again and I am well.

GANYMEDE. O glorious Pagod, roundly Rump, grant my Requeſt and ſee that *Polecat* the Magician die!

The Rump farts.

MAGICIAN. But now, I have the Ring and no Requeſt of mine may be refuſed! Two of us can play at this.

The Magician *goes to the Idol.* Ganymede *retreats.*

O groſs, great Rump, of goldly Hue, grant my Wiſh for Mercy and Leniency and let me live.

The Rump farts.

GANYMEDE. O Rump, how can you thus refuſe me?

PRIESTESS. It is too well known that when two Wiſhes fall in conflict, it goes to the Preſs and then to the Coffee-Houſes where it is diſcuſſed to Death and all forgotten.

MAGICIAN. Ay, or elſe 'tis left to the King's deciſion — which is why I aſk a new Favour with my Ring. O grand glorious greatly golden globulous Rump, I aſk that as the King is forever in *Sauſageland* and unable to ſerve, I be made King inſtead.

The Rump farts. Enter Courtiers *with Crown. They put it upon the* Magician *and dance around him.*

COURTIER 1. Our new King is declared!

COURTIER 2. Long live the King!

They hum ZADOK THE PRIEST.

PRIESTESS. *Ganymede*! Uſe your Favour, find ſome Way to undo this!

GANYMEDE. O big and brightly Bottom, glorious golden Rump, I beg — let there be a Riot and the King overthrown by the People!

The Rump farts. The hummed tune changes to DOWN AMONG THE DEAD MEN, *and the* Courtiers *cloſe violently upon the* Magician.

MAGICIAN. O! O! Alas and alack, I am killed! Curſe you *Ganymede!* Curſe you and all the World from *Wales* to *Hannover!*

Magician *lies dead.*

FOYST. In my far off foreign Land, when Men of great Power die, we eat their Bodies to abſorb their Power.

COURTIER 1. That ſounds a ſplendid Notion. Friends let us cut him up and eat his Body, as do the wiſe Slaves.

The Courtiers *begin to cut up and eat the body of the* Magician.

COURTIER 2. There is Blood enough for Years of Black Pudding within this great Gut.

COURTIER 3. His Entrails are so filled with fragrant Dung! It is delicious!

Enter a Meſſenger.

MESSENGER. What ho, to whom do I give my Meſſage? Who holds Power in this Court?

PRIESTESS. I am High Prieſteſs, deliver News to me.

MESSENGER. I am come from *Sauſageland* with devaſtating News. The good King *Piles* of *Groſſ-Corruptia* hath periſhed in a Banquet from eating too many Sauſages. *Per* his wiſhes, he ſhall be interred in his Homeland of *Sauſageland*, which he always lov'd the beſt.

PRIESTESS. Did he leave no Heirs?

MESSENGER. Only of a natural ſort.

PRIESTESS. Then it is for me to decide our next King. *Ganymede*, for your loyal Service and for the fineneſs of your Arſe which goes unrivalled, I ſay that you ſhall be our new King in *Groſſ-Corruptia*. Do you accept the Honour?

GANYMEDE. By the flying Fundament, I do!

PRIESTESS. Then let us crown him.

The Courtiers *riſe and put the Crown on him, and circle him whilſt humming* ZADOK THE PRIEST.

And you muſt complete the Ceremony by taking up a ſnow white male Swan, forcing Chriſtian ſacramental Bread up his Fundament, buggering him with your Prick, and then as you fire off your ſteaming Shot within him you ſhall ſtrangle him dead. So goes the Antient Rite.

Two Slaves *bring out a Swan, and* Ganymede *performs the Ceremony while the* Courtiers *continue to hum the Tune around him.*

FINIS.

AUTHOR'S NOTES.

I don't remember how I first stumbled across the Wikipedia page for *The Golden Rump*, but as soon as I heard the basics of the story — that it was an obscene 18th century play probably written by the Prime Minister of Great Britain — I began thinking of how to make a novel out of it. I did a great deal more research, the most useful sources being the book entitled *The Licensing Act of 1737* by Vincent J. Liesenfeld, and the paper by Peter Thomson, called *Fielding, Walpole, George II and the Liberty of the Theatre*. I also made use of many primary sources, such as the magazine *Common Sense* which furnished the basic details of *The Golden Rump's* original plot.

I had originally conceived the story of *Slick Filth* as a novel which would follow Walpole as he tried to compose the play, and my idea was to include occasional excerpts of what he was writing, which would amount to the entire play being shown in pieces. I wrote the reconstructed *Golden Rump*, using the known information about it. As there isn't very much surviving material, I took most of the premise from the story of *Aladdin*; and as it was my mission to write the *filthiest play ever* as conceived in 1737, I not only looked at controversial plays of the 18th century such as *Pasquin* and *The Beggar's Opera*, but also the modern film reputed to be the filthiest thing ever made, *Pink Flamingos*. It is worth noting that *Pink Flamingos* was not considerably worse than some of the actual historical materials my research uncovered, such as the play *Sodom, or; The Quintessence of Debauchery*, a genuine stage instruction from which is:

ACTUS QUINTUS
[A grove of cypress and other trees cut in shapes of pricks. Several arbours, figures, and pleasant ornaments. In a banqueting-house are discovered men playing on tabours and dulcimers with their pricks, and women with jews' harps in their cunts.]

In any case, I wrote *The Golden Rump's* script to my satisfaction; I then began to work on the novel, wrote one chapter that wasn't very good, and having no better ideas for it gave it up for about a year, during which

I instead wrote *Molly Brazen, The Sentimental Pervert, A Devil Put Aside,* some revisions to *Steps of the Malefactor*, and some screenplays.

The following year I came across the *Golden Rump* script again, and I was actually impressed with how correctly I'd imitated the style of early 18th century plays, and by the number of obscure historical references I'd worked into it (and some modern ones — Priestess Messalina is obviously being played by Mae West in my mind.) This inspired me to give another try to the novel; but after some thought I realized that the story was not really rich enough to be worth a novel's length, and that it was more likely to succeed as a short story that would serve as an introduction to the play script. I quickly found that the mysterious Henry Giffard turned himself into the hero of the story, and after the first draft I rewrote it to be told from his viewpoint.

Henry Giffard's name comes up in discussions of *The Golden Rump* as its possible author (Henry Fielding being another one often proposed) but while it seems that everyone who has looked into the matter agrees that Robert Walpole himself somehow arranged the writing of the play or possibly even wrote it himself, no real information or proof of it survives; which perhaps classifies this whole story as an Alternate History or a Secret History. There's not a great deal of information about the real Henry Giffard as a person, either. It's known that he was a professional actor, married to a professional actress. He owned stakes in various theatres, performed in various shows, and in the 1730s took over the theatre at Goodman's-Fields in what was then a rather sketchy part of London, right on the outskirts of the city. Walpole's Licensing Act ruined this theatre (as it was not able to procure a License, and by 1741 it was referred to as "the late Theatre in Goodman's-Fields") but Giffard kept it running for a while using various loopholes in the law, for instance offering his plays as "free entertainment" while finding other excuses to make people pay for entry. He's notable for having discovered the actor David Garrick, whose stage debut was at Goodman's-Fields.

The only sample of Giffard's writing I was able to find was a theatrical adaptation of Samuel Richardson's 1740 book *Pamela.*

Giffard converted the epistolary novel into a suitable stageplay, then had it performed at Goodman's-Fields with himself as Mr. B and his wife as Pamela. It seems that Giffard retired from acting sometime in the 1750s, and died in 1772. That's as much as I know about him, and about as much as anyone knows of him.

For the language, when writing *The Golden Rump* I used Henry Fielding's plays as my primary model; though I recognize a lot of imitation of John Gay's writing tone. For Giffard's story, I had originally used Eliza Haywood's *Jemmy and Jenny Jessamy* for my linguistic model (she actually makes an uncredited appearance in *Slick Filth*, as one of the players on stage in *The Historical Register of 1736*, in which she was a real-life actor.) When I later located Giffard's version of *Pamela*, I adjusted the writing to better reflect his actual style.

The print book of *Slick Flith* is designed to resemble authentic books of the 18th century. The trim size is based on an 18th century play-book; the primary body font, Broadsheet by 3IP (www.3ip.com), has been carefully chosen to match what was used in real books of the time; the peculiar spelling and punctuation of the era has been matched to the best of my ability; and I have troubled to introduce a few errors in the "typesetting" since I am amused to see a sort of error in old books which is peculiar to them, namely of letters being put in upside-down by mistake. I tried to follow the unofficial "rules" of the long-S as declared by the internet, even though I have seen real period books that use them otherwise. Exceptions to these rules were sometimes made for readability's sake.

As always, Google Books and the Online Etymology Dictionary (www.etymonline.com) have been extremely useful in my attempts to double-check my attempts at historical language.

Slick Filth:
A story of Robert Walpole and Henry Giffard, to which is Appended the Farce of The Golden Rump.

www.ingramcontent.com/pod-product-compliance
Lightning Source LLC
Chambersburg PA
CBHW030601310726
48979CB00003B/526

* 9 7 8 1 7 3 4 1 8 4 6 2 4 *